Praise for

Jack and the
Bear Scarin' Socks
and Other Tales

Doug Jones, a master storyteller, captures audiences with his delightful Jack Tales. The adventures he weaves catapult the reader, keeping them curious and laughing out loud. Mischief greets you on every page. Each Jack Tale sweeps the reader along on a cultural heritage journey through hollers where critters' voices surprise you with hilarity when least expected. The warmth Jones exudes makes me eager to introduce Jack Tales to new generations in my family whom I trust will beg me to repeat them each time we gather. Having the good fortune to hear Jones spin his Jack Tales in person, I highly recommend you invite him to reunions or any time you want to transport and treat your guests.

—**Evelyn Asher, Author,**
What She Carries: A poetic memoir.

Readers of all ages—prepare to be carried away to an Appalachian community, a place where young Jack encounters *stitch-u-ayshuns* that evolve into life lessons. You will be captivated by the colorful characters, authentic dialog and the wisdom of the local folk. These short stories are masterfully told! You will learn about what makes the cove _the cove,_ and much, much more. Reading through these fables your eyes will open to a part of Americana that most people never experience. There's a lesson cleverly woven into each tale that gives pause to ponder. This collection never fails to delight with its colorful images, lively characters, and life lessons. A clever, entertaining, one-of-a-kind book.

—Charlene DeWitt, Author & Editor,
Past VP – NE Georgia Writers

Doug Jones spins a series of heartwarming tales about young Jack and his adventures in the Appalachian Mountains. These exploits take Jack all over the hills and vales of Brooks Cove where he encounters all sorts of characters and critters—most benevolent, but others not so much. The backdrop of the Appalachians shapes these adventures and provides the context for Jack's life lessons. Come along with Jack to visit a simpler time and place, and to gain a richer appreciation of deeper values.

—Jim Brown, Emeritus Professor

One of the tales in this collection, _Jack and the Piebald Ridge Deer,_ touched me like no other. The tale is like the Piebald deer herself—a rare and beautiful treasure. The story is obviously written with deep love and respect for the Appalachian culture and its place in the history of this land. The language is rich, colorful and evocative. In the written dialect, I can hear the people speaking and though it's different from the way I speak, it sings of place and relationship. This Jack tale teaches us about the importance of place and all that entails to our sense of self;

in essence we belong to our ancient lands and all the creatures thereon. The interweaving of place, history and relationships shows us the Cove as Beloved Community.

—**Rev. Christine Jones-Leavy**

JACK AND THE
BEAR SCARIN' SOCKS
AND OTHER TALES

JACK AND THE
BEAR SCARIN' SOCKS
AND OTHER TALES

Jim & Diana —
Thank you for your acclamation,
your encouragement, and your
appreciation of High Country culture.
And most of all, thank you for your
abiding friendship.

"There's always more to the story..."
— *Doug* 2-1-2023

Doug Jones

***BOOK*LOGIX®**
Alpharetta, GA

ISBN: 978-1-6653-0516-7 - Paperback
eISBN: 978-1-6653-0517-4 - eBook

Library of Congress Control Number: 2022922171

♾This paper meets the requirements of ANSI/NISO Z39.48-1992 (Permanence of Paper)

120122

Dedicated to my wife Pam
and our children Nathan, and Lauren

Each of you shows up as the inspiration for characters, for
"sitch-u-ations," and for lessons learned in these tales.
And, more importantly, each of you has supported me by
offering your thoughtful feedback while I was writing,
your twinkling eyes and willing ears as I was learning to
tell these tales, and your unconditional love.
My family truly is a gift from God.

Your support has made these tales worth telling "outside
the cove."

Contents

Map of Brooks Cove

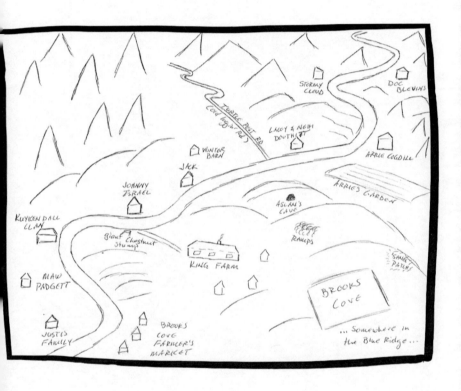

Residents of Brooks Cove

- Dean Justis family
- Olivia "Maw" Padgett (husband: Samuel, deceased, children Erin, Roy, Cara)
- the Kuykendall clan (6 children, including Tom, inlaws and outlaws)
- Farmer King family (2 sons and their families, 1 unmarried daughter. Large farming operation)
- Johnny Israel (wife: Lisa, deceased)
- Jack and his family, Mother: Dayle, Father: Lee, Grandmother: Eulagene, Dog: Angelo
- Lacey and Nehi Douthitt
- Arrie Cogdill
- Stormy Cloud (Wife: Angelina, deceased)
- Doc Blevins (Wife: Pauline, deceased)

- … and, of course, Aslan

Introduction

"Y'all ain't gonna believe this, but it's true ..."

That's how each tale in this collection begins, and with good reason. Storytelling is foundational for the preservation of every culture, and in Southern Appalachia, storytelling is not only an art form, it's an important part of everyday communication. Whether your story is told in a general store on a Tuesday night in July or read in a school gymnasium in Rabun Gap with young'uns scattered around on sit-upons; whether it's polished and published in a fancy-covered book or just barely tolerated in family traditions, it's the *tales* in a culture that make that culture memorable, warts 'n all. Usually there's an element of truth to accompany the typical exaggeration, and when you're really connected to the story's teller, the story goes far beyond the words, touching your heart, illuminating your mind, and providing discernment that enriches your life. Jack Tales, told well, do all of that.

So how do you tell a *Tale* well? One Tuesday night in July, a year after our family moved to the High Country of North Carolina, we ventured to a local general store for *Storytellin' Night* to see how it's done. We bought our supper, a cold cola in a glass bottle in one hand with the requisite hot dog in the other. We plopped ourselves down on barrels and wooden boxes and proceeded to have the most delightful of evenings! Over the years that we lived in the High Country, we sought out story tellers at festivals, paid attention when we learned a storyteller's books were to be featured at a literary event, and tuned our ears to learn as much as we could about Jack Tales and wooly worm caterpillers, about legends and oddities, and about colorful High Country dialect.

So, when we headed up to participate in a family camp weekend just over the border in Tennessee, a pair of dirty white socks laying in the middle of a camp road was not wasted on me. The seed was planted for what has become the first tale in this book and the creation of a community I dubbed Brooks Cove and a leading character named Jack.

In the process of writing these stories, I learned all I could about Jack Tales. Even though the most widely known Jack Tales, like "Jack and the Beanstalk" (*folk in Appalachia call it "Jack and the Bean Tree"*) or "Jack the Giant Killer," have roots in Great Britain, lots of Jack Tales arose in Southern Appalachian culture and became more widely known because in the late 1930s and 1940s Richard Chase had the good sense to seek out and transcribe the tales told by story tellers in the Blue Ridge mountains. A good Southern Appalachian Jack Tale is told in the native tongue – a derivative of Scottish and the Olde English of the common folk. It's the preservation of the form and context of a Tale told in authentic dialect that makes it compelling.

I have come to understand that there are some "rules" for telling Jack Tales:

> Rule Number 1 (for storytellers): If you're telling a Southern Appalachian story, like a Jack Tale, you have to speak the language. In particular, you have to say, "cain't", "don'tcha know", "fixin' t'" or "whatchacall" at least

once in the story and draw upon a colorful phrase or colloquial description – y' know, one that someone inside the culture would use naturally, but one that someone "off the mountain" would notice and either scratch his head or think it's cute or funny.

Rule Number 2 (for listeners): Don't judge the intelligence of the characters nor the wisdom of the tale by the dialect in which it is told or written. Wisdom and significance are related more to the intentionality of being thoughtful, resourceful, and respectful than they are to the diplomas and degrees that follow the author's name. Being able to connect to the audience is far more important than being able to impress them with an academic pedigree.

Jack Tales always center on a boy by the name of Jack and resemble an "everyman" tale. Jack always gets himself into trouble of some kind and the tale follows how he gets out of trouble, usually having bettered his own situation. The classic Jack Tales have Jack saving himself because he is a trickster, a thief, or an opportunist.

The tales in this book all take place "Somewhere in the Blue Ridge" mountains of Southern Appalachia in a fictional place called Brooks Cove. Jack is, of course, the center attraction of each tale, and the people of the cove show up in various tales with typical southern Appalachian names. This collection contains a hand-drawn map of Brooks Cove and a list of residents of the Cove. But Jack as a trickster or thief? These tales will have none of that. Jack still gets into trouble, and he still gets out of trouble. But in this collection, Jack is helped, sometimes from the "critters" of the cove, sometimes by a person from the cove, and sometimes by Divine intervention. Various tales in this collection reveal some of Jack's history and why it is so important that Jack is *"not a trickster nor a thief."*

Each tale has something in it that connects to my own personal experience – it's up to you to guess what that connection is – and each took on a life of its own while being written. Although it usually was the case that I knew something of how Jack was going to land in trouble while I was in the early stages of writing the tale, sometimes I didn't know how he was going to be rescued until it was nearly accomplished. And in at least one tale, I didn't know the full nature of the significance of the tale until after I had finished writing the last word. Talk about a humbling experience.

"So pull up a chair and put y'r listening ears on and get y'rself ready for some storytellin'. Y'r life's about to get a leeetle bit better."

—dj
Gainesville, GA

Jack and the Bear-Scarin' Socks

*Y'all ain't gonna b'lieve this,
but it's true – at least as true as a Jack Tale oughta be ...*

"Daddy, how come we're goin' over t' Cove Creek f'r fam'ly camp?" Jack wadn't sure he wanted t' go.

"Got m' reasons." Mr. Lee, Jack's daddy, was surprised at Jack's reluctance. "Why? You know they's a little bit o' fam'ly history up there. You got somethin' better t' do?"

"No, sir. It's just that me an' Will was..."

"*Will and I were*," Jack's mama, Miss Dayle, was a stickler f'r good grammar even though she spoke the typical High Country dialect of Brooks Cove.

"*Will and I were* gonna go on a 'ad-venture' on Saturday. We was goin' t' take the Cove Road on up past Doc Blevins' place."

"Doc's place ain't goin' nowhere. It'll still be here next week," said Jack's daddy. "It's June – school's out; you and Will c'n take y'r 'ad-venture' next week. Cove Creek Camp'll be good f'r us. Mr. Nate's 'spectin' us and a few other fam'lies. His cookin' will change y'r mind, certain-sure. AND, I was talkin' to 'im th'other day an' he said he'll have some special activities ready f'r us. Never know what y'll see up in th' High Country -- the Camp is kindly large."

* * *

Brooks Cove is nestled somewhere in the High Country of the Blue Ridge Mountains in the Southern Appalachians. Cove Creek Camp was a ways on north from Brooks Cove; Jack had never been there. Fact is, Mr. Lee and Miss Dayle had met at Cove Creek Family Camp 20 years ago. Mr. Lee had made special plans f'r an anniversary o' sorts.

So, on Friday afternoon, Jack an' his Mama and Daddy arrived at the top o' the camp, ready for a special weekend. Upon gettin' checked in they were directed down a camp road t' get set up. After Jack helped his Daddy set up their tent, he was ready for supper, but it was a whole hour till it was gonna be ready.

"Mama, can I go on back up t' the lodge? I can meet y' up there for supper. I'll bet they's somethin' int'restin' on the way, and I 'spect they might be other young'uns up there."

"We'll see y' there. Don't get distracted." Jack's Mama knew her son well. She knew he'd be safe, and this trip was as much for Jack as it was for her and Lee. "I'll get our 'vacation home' prettied up and talk t' some o' th' other Mamas."

Wellsir, Jack took off up the mountain toward the top o' the cove again. It was a few stone's throws up that rattly old hardscrabble road t' the lodge where supper was goin' to be, but Jack, he didn't mind the road, it wadn't much different from the one goin' t' his Mamaw Eulagene's place. As he was gettin' up toward the top, he spied what *used t' be* a pair o' white socks just a lyin' in the middle o' the road. They wadn't nobody else around, and the socks looked like they had been just a lyin' there for a while; so, bein' a boy, Jack just let 'em lie. You could tell they used t' be white, but just barely. Kindly reminds me o' a song *my* young'uns used t' sing with their mama. You remind me, and I'll sing it for y' 'nother time.

* * *

As supper was finishin' up, Mr. Nate got folks' attention. "Thank y'all f'r comin' t' our annual Cove Creek Fam'ly camp. If you've been here b'fore, it's good t' see y' again. Iff'n y'r new t' Cove Creek Camp, I'm proud t' meet y'. A few things b'fore y'all head back down t' y'r campsites. 1. Breakfast will be at 8:00 sharp. It's worth bein' on time – y'all already know that breakfast is much better hot than cold. 2. Since last year, we've got us a couple o' dogs – Snickers an' Angelo – an' I hope you make their acquaintance. They're right friendly with campers, so no worries there. 3. Feel free t' stay up here at the lodge as long as y' want. Lights will go out at 10:30, and we've got a few extra flashlights if y' want one for goin' back t' your tent sites."

"Lee," whispered Miss Dayle, "I overheard some o' the others say that they's bears up here in the camp. Do y' think we'll be safe?"

"I'm sure it'll be fine, Darlin'. High Country bears don't go lookin' f'r trouble. Prob'ly the reason f'r th' dogs. You know Nate -- if there was any reason t' be concerned, he woulda tol' us. I reckon those dogs got a *understandin'* with the bears."

* * *

Jack woke up early the next mornin' an' started up the road quiet like so's he wouldn't disturb anybody. Part way up, he spied them socks still layin' there.

"Well I'll be. Sure as dawn streamin' through th' balsams they wadn't left by one o' Mamaw Eulagene's kin. She'd a had whoever left 'em doin' laundry for the whole camp!" But, Jack didn't pick 'em up neither. Continuing up the road, he thought t' himself, "*Sure hope Mr. Nate's gettin' breakfast ready. I'm starvin!*"

Right when Jack was thinkin' 'bout bein' hungry, he looked up and saw a black bear yonder up in the middle o' that self-same road. He stopped short. "At least it ain't no mama bear – that's good. But he ain't no cub neither. From the look of it, he's a teenager. That might not be good. Doc Blevins says that when nobody's watchin' 'em, teenage boys do stupid stuff."

So, Jack was a little afraid, but he was hungry, and breakfast was gonna be up at the lodge. So he trudged on up the road anyway. The bear was hungry, too, and he came on down the road, thinkin' that he might have *his* breakfast courtesy o' Jack. When he wadn't but a few yards from Jack, he stopped cold and they faced off.

(*Now, y'all know they ain't nothin' good'll come from teenage boys tied up in a "hungry" contest.*)

In a fit o' inspiration, Jack high-tailed it down the road with the bear in hot pursuit. He nigh-on stumbled over them socks he had NOT picked up earlier. Bein' from the High Country, Jack knew all about a bear's sense o' smell. All's he could think t' do was t' grab them filthy stinkin' socks and shove 'em at that boy-bear's nose and hope it worked.

"Take that, you long-nosed nary-a-tail critter!" Jack couldn't resist the urge t' insult the bear. But he also cried out, "Lord save me!" He squeezed his eyes shut, expectin' the worst! Completely befuddled, Jack looked up as the bear screeched to a halt, then turned an' raced off the road, past the tents over on the right, and off through a rhododendron thicket only a bear could bust through! But just b'fore he got the big head for grabbin' them *bear-scarin' socks*, out the corner o' his eye, Jack could hear somethin' else a chasin' that bear—Angelo the bear-despisin', people-pr'tectin' camp dog!

Jack realized that when the bear looked at him a-holdin' them socks, what he really saw was that dog, and rather than gettin' into a fight with a territorial, camp-pr'tectin' dog, the bear decided to, shall we say, *re-evaluate* and avoid the situation. It was a good decision.

After a short spell, Jack saw Angelo headed back t' camp. He ran t' get 'im, rubbed 'im b'hind his ears. "Angelo, you saved my life! Let's go see if Mr. Nate got any breakfast ready. You deserve my share for what you done."

Angelo looked up at Jack and said, "Y'r welcome.

'twarn't nothin'. I got a camp t' pr'tect, and that boy-bear was getting' in the way. Ever'body that come up here t' my home -- I got their back. An' I like it like 'at."

Jack felt special, Angelo talkin' t' him. "Me, too, Angelo. I like it like 'at, too. Now let's go find ol' Nate and get us some breakfast."

Jack and the Flea-Fleein' Coyote

Y'all ain't gonna b'lieve this, but it's true, at least as true as a Jack Tale oughta be...

I heard it direc'ly from Jack only a month or so after it happened. A word ahead o'time. A lot had happened since Jack nearly b'come breakfast for a teenage boy-bear up at Cove Creek Camp. One thing y'all will notice is that now Angelo, the dog who saved Jack from the bear, had

7

come t' live with Jack's family. Ol' Nate --the chef from Cove Creek Camp-- he knew all about the *sitch-u-ayshun* with the bear and saw how Angelo and Jack hit it off. He learn't that Jack didn't have no dog –said it was near criminal for a boy in the High Country t' not have a dog. Nate decided t' let Angelo go off and pr'tect Jack's family here in Brooks Cove. Th'other thing you'll figger out is that it ain't just a narrator's thing—havin' critters talk. It truly ain't uncommon for folk in *Appalachia* t' speak t' critters and have 'em speak back. Mebbe the critters can talk, mebbe they cain't. In these stories, some of 'em do – and s'rprisin'ly, some of 'em don't. Well, on with the tale.

Jack was wanderin' out in the Cove one day, nothin' particular in mind. "Hey, Will." Jack spied his friend from down the mountain.

"Hey, Jack." Will prob'ly didn't have nothin' on his mind, neither. Jack and Will were 'occasional' friends from school and were known t' fish and wander together. Usually, they didn't get int' *sitch-u-ayshuns* together, but they also didn't, shall we say, *inspire* each other t' do what they were s'posed t' do. Sometimes, after they were together, Jack was slow t' do what he promised his Daddy he'd do, and instead said som'thin' like "I'll do it, Daddy, I will." Mr. Lee, was fond of sayin' back t' him, "*Will* ain't y'r friend." Drove Jack crazy, but he reckoned he had it comin'. Still, Will and Jack *were* friends and liked t' do stuff together.

"Wanna go on a *ad-venture*?"

Will always liked t' go on an adventure with Jack. "Sure! Where d'ya wanna go?"

"Don't make no never mind. Let's go up the ol' loggin' road and see what we c'n see up in the meadow."

Will hadn't ever been up t' the meadow b'fore, but he

was certain sure Jack had been up there. Jack had been ever'where up in the Cove. So Jack and Will took off – two boys from the High Country with some clear blue sky and a slight breeze clamberin' around the mountains up above Brooks Cove. Don't get no better'n 'at.

They each picked up a stick – a boy cain't go wanderin' without a proper stick – and headed up the ol' loggin road, then hooked up with an old Cherokee trail from two hunnerd years ago when they was thousands o' Cherokee in the High Country. That trail took 'em up t' the meadow. Now b'tween you an' me it wadn't no story-book meadow, like them Grimm fellers would-a tol' about, but it *was* a clearin'—nigh onto a bald—and Jack liked sayin' the word "meadow." So Jack and Will -- they was in a meadow.

"I'm tard, Jack." Will didn't go wanderin' as much as Jack, an' he was ready for a rest.

"It's a pull comin' up that last part t' the meadow. Y' c'n lay down fer a spell, Will, iff'n y'need t' rest." Neither of 'em brought ary a snack, but it didn't matter, they was on a 'ad-venture!'

Jack *didn't* say he was kindly tired too, but he was. Both of 'em got comf'terble up at the edge of that high meadow, lay their sticks down beside of 'em, and quickly went dreamy-like. In what seemed like only a couple o' minutes, Jack woke up. Bein' a mountain boy out on the mountain, he had enough sense t' not just get up real sudden-like. It was late afternoon, and lookin' around, he saw over yonder 'cross th' clearin' a coyote doin' coyote things. About that time, the coyote spied Jack 'n Will and started creeping in their direction.

Jack studied the coyote for a minute. "Will. It's Diablo."
"What's Diablo?"
"That coyote over yonder. He's comin' toward us. I

recognize 'im from what Mr. Israel don' tol' me about 'im last week." Johnny Israel was one o' Jack's neighbors. He had chickens and rabbits and kindly kept an eye out for other critters that was lookin' for a free meal.

"Mr. Israel tol' me that Diablo – what he *called* that rascal *–was* kinda mean and devilish an' I should watch out fer 'im if I go up the ol' Cherokee trail."

For those who ain't been around coyotes, they's no more like dogs than that yellow velvet-melty stuff is like real cheese! They *are* kindly sneaky, but they definitely ain't the bumblin' idiots they was made out t' be on them old *Road Runner* cartoons. Mr. Israel tol' me that coyotes are newcomers t' the Blue Ridge – they wadn't up here when he was comin' on. So, they's kindly unpredictable. On the other hand, they are *very* opportunistic, and that rubbed Jack the wrong way.

"Coyotes don't generally hunt large critters unless they're starvin', Will, and when they hunt small critters, they's always alone. They ain't no reason for ary critter t' go hungry up here in the High Country, so Diablo's prob'ly alone." Jack knew t' keep his eyes on Diablo, starin' 'im down. Diablo seen 'im and returned the stare. It was a cold look.

"I'm gettin' my stick, Jack. Just in case." Will didn't know what he'd do with it, but he felt better havin' a stick than havin' nothin' but his wits.

"Good idea." Jack secretly thought that when it come t' bein' prepared for *sitch-u-ayshuns*, Will wadn't the sharpest knife in th' drawer. "Keep an eye on 'im, Will, whilst I get ready, too. Just stare at 'im. We'll show Diablo we ain't scared." Will wadn't so sure, but he stared hard at that coyote.

Jack wadn't necessarily afraid of a single coyote, but he didn't like the idea of being close t' one. They's kind of – well let's just say they ain't got much hygiene. And, Jack knew that if ol' Diablo came after 'em, not bein' critters a coyote would hunt naturally, they'd need t' at least wonder if that filthy scavenger had the hydrophobie (that's *rabies* for you non-Ol'Yellar folk). "At least Diablo ain't got no foamy mouth. We c'n handle 'im, Will."

Jack took his eyes off of Ol' Diablo for a second t' get his stick, and in that time, Diablo d'cided t' come see what kind of trouble he could stir up.

"Jack! He's comin'! Diablo's comin'! What'll we do?!"

When Jack looked up, here come that mangy cur tearin' toward 'em like his tail was on fire! "Act like y'r crazy, Will. Don't hold back." They started hollerin' and runnin' around, tryin' t' make it look like they was more'n just the two of 'em. Jack knew they couldn't outrun Diablo, and he was more'n sorry Angelo was workin' f'r Jack's Daddy and couldn't come with 'em--Angelo had stared down **bears** on the mountain before and wouldn't be afraid of a measly coyote. But Angelo wadn't there, and Diablo sure didn't seem t' be bothered by Jack an' Will's jumpin' and hollerin.' He just kep' on comin' like he didn't even hear 'em. When he was getting close t' Jack an' Will, Diablo growled, "Prepare t' meet y'r maker!"

Lucky fer them, Rex the flea had been follerin' Jack an' Will most of the day. Turns out that Friday a week 'r two ago --- *Pardon me, I feel a distraction comin' on, tellin' y' about Rex. Ask me later, an' I'll fill y' in on Rex the flea an' his jumpin' ability. I cain't leave Jack and Will now – look like Diablo's 'bout t' get 'em!*

"Will! We got t' stop runnin' an' jumpin' an' hollerin.'" Turnin' t' Rex, Jack said, " 'at there's the best meal you'll get today, Rex. Sic 'em, an' may God go with you."

Just as Diablo was gettin' ready t' pounce on Jack, Rex jumped one o' his championship jumps and quickly worked hisself down t' Diablo's back, right where he knew

Diablo couldn't reach t' scratch at 'im. Jack stared up at ol' Diablo and simply said, "I'm a gonna resist you, Diablo. Bring it if y' dare, but I'm standin' firm. If you got ary sense, you'll turn tail an' run. Just know a giant of a jumper is on your back an' you done already lost *this* fight."

Diablo, he was puzzled, but in a New York minute, he realized Rex had done got t' work. He was itchin' worse'n he ever done itched b'fore an' he couldn't scratch it. He started whinin' so bad it'd make a spoiled baby jealous. Diablo found out he'd been bested. He suddenly lost interest in Jack an' Will, turned his tail, an' started t' flea – er, f-l-double-ee.

"'at 'air's how y' deal with a coyote, Will."

"Wow, Jack. I ain't never seen nothin' like 'at before. Mebbe I should go get some fleas fer myself, y' know, when we go on other *ad-ventures*."

"Be careful, Will. Don't let y'r Mama know. Mamas don't understand such things like us boys do. Wanna come home an' have supper with us? Mama'll be glad t' have you, an' Daddy c'n take ya t' your own house after we eat. You c'n tell your family about our ad-venture."

"When we get t' y'r house, Jack, let me call 'em, t' see if it'll be ok."

"Sure, Will. I know it'll be fine."

Jack an' Will, calm as they could be, made their way back down the mountain t' the ol' loggin' road so's they could get home for supper. First thing Jack said when they got there was, "Mama, Daddy – Will and me learned what they meant in church a few weeks ago. You 'member the preacher read from the book of James, 'Resist the devil and he will flee.' Who'd a knowed he was spellin' it 'f-l-double-e' an' not 'f-l-e-a'. You cain't possibly know just how true that scripture is."

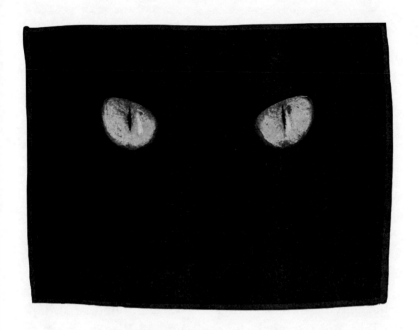

Jack and
the Cave Eyes

Y'all ain't gonna b'lieve this,
but it's true, at least as true as a Jack Tale oughta be...

Jack done tol' me about it only about a hour after it happened, and then he took me t' the place where he done got scareder than he had been the first time he stared down a black bear up at Cove Creek Camp.

Wellsir, Jack heard tell that his neighbor up in Brooks

Cove, Farmer King, had lost livestock lately due t' who knows what and that he was offerin' a reward t' whoever could clear it up and make the King farm safe again. Not knowin' the size of the reward nor the risk of meetin' up with whatever was messin' with the livestock, Jack thought he'd go over t' the King farm and see what he could find out. Farmer King was, by cove standards, a rich man, but he was so prideful it left a bad smell in your nose whene'er you was near his farm. Jack didn't like him, but mebbee it'd be a right good reward –Jack never turned down no reward. Bein' a little cautious, Jack stuffed a pair of ol' socks in his pocket and took a few fleas off'n Angelo the bear-scarin' dog and put 'em in a jar "just in case."

On his way over t' see Farmer King, Jack took a shortcut through the woods. He figgered he might find a patch of wild 'sang (ginseng), dig some up and then sell it off t' some fancy "health food store" or tourist. Mr. Justis done tol' him that 'sang brought a good price. After a few minutes studyin' the woods, he looked up and saw a cave over yonder. Jack didn't remember seein' that partic'lar cave b'fore, and, bein' a boy, he was curious and thought he'd go over and take a look. He clambered up t' the mouth of that cave and without thinking (that was a real problem for Jack), he poked his own head in the front of the cave and said, "Boo." *Then* he looked in. He'd a-jumped outta his socks if he was wearin' any. Right there, not 5 feet in front of him in that dark cave was 2 greenish-goldish eyes lookin' right back at him. They made nary a sound, so Jack knew right away it warn't no milk cow nor goat nor chicken, but the way them eyes looked – why Jack was cold all the way down his spine. It chilled him t' the bone an' he lit out on toward Farmer King's place.

Whilst he was, shall we say 'engineerin' his escape from

them cave eyes, Jack started t' relive that experience, tryin' t' figger out what surprised him so much. Bein' a mountain boy up in the High Country, Jack done heared of all kinds of wild animals holin' up in caves, but he hadn't quite knowed where those caves was. Now, in the light of them cave eyes, he *was* sure he'd found at least one o' them caves, and he was certain-sure he'd found one o' them wild animals.

Jack's mind started racin' through the list of critters it could be – black bear? 'coon? catamount? (For the un-mountainish out there, catamount, or "cat-of-the-mountain" is another name for a mountain lion.) Jack didn't even consider the little critters like squirrels and sally-manders. But he DID remember hearin' that his papaw's papaw done tol' of someone long ago tellin' about seein' a *Yayhoo* hidin' out on the mountain. Don't nobody know for sure what a *Yayhoo* is nor what it looks like, but they all agree that it's scary. And Jack also heard tell of a giant *Dwayyo* – a kind of wolf-man standin' up on his hind legs as tall as a chestnut sapling.

I know that all y'all think I'm a makin' this stuff up, but I ain't. Check it out y'self if you've got the courage -- mountain lore don't survive for generations without it bein' true enough.

Jack got scareder and scareder as he thought about them creatures and what might be behind those cave eyes. But he'd done had his experience with a bear, and wadn't so scared of one of them no more – less'n it was a mama bear with cubs. And, he'd had t' chase coons away from his porch when they took t' tryin' t' steal cookies and pies off the rail. He forced himself t' not even consider the idea of a unknown *Yayhoo*, and if a 7-foot tall *Dwayyo* was *anything* like a overgrowed coyote, well he had his fleas in a jar t' take care of him. Anyways, Jack couldn't conjure up no idee of them monsters hidin' quiet-like in a cave nor being any good as a livestock thief. But a catamount? Now that fit.

Because of them eyes, Jack hurried on over t' the King farm t' get the scoop on the livestock gone missin' and find out what the reward was. When he asked, Farmer King tol' him that the reward was $1000. (Seem like Kingly rewards is always $1000 in Jack Tales!) King said, "I'm a thinkin' it's that varmint catamount that folks has heard prowlin' around lookin' for somethin' t' devour. So iff'n you want the reward, I'll pay you in cash money when you either bring back the missin' livestock or the carcass of the critter that done took 'em."

Now that there was a lot of cash money, so there wadn't nothin' for Jack t' do but t' take on the challenge. He told King, tryin' t' impress 'im, "You need t' start gettin' that reward money ready. I'll be back tomorrow t' collect on it." King said, "It'll be ready, but iff'n you don't want t' be laughed at by the whole cove (Farmer King had the big head – just 'cause his name was King, he thought he was the King of the cove), you better be ready t' meet my terms." Jack said back at him, "Time's a wastin'. I'll see y'uns b'fore sundown tomorrow." And off he took.

Now, whilst he was a jawin' with King, Jack's mind kep' goin' back t' the cave and the catamount. He was certain-sure it was a catamount, because of how its eyes looked, but he was also sure that ol' wildcat warn't the varmint responsible for King's missin' livestock. Since it had NOT chased after him when he surprised it earlier in the day, and since Jack knowed that its claws was NOT, as his MaMaw used t' say, "dull as a ol' fro," Jack began t' calc'late - maybe, just maybe, that catamount would help 'im get Farmer King's reward.

So, Jack scurried back t' the cave where the eyes had been earlier in the day and, carefully this time, inched up closer t' the mouth of the cave. He started by sayin', "Catamount, I know you're in there, and I know you got noble character. Ol' Farmer King done made a big deal about his missin' livestock, and he says it was you who took 'em. But just 2 days ago, *after* the reward was announced, Tom done seen him at the feed store pickin' up a load of livestock feed. They's somethin' that ain't quite right."

The Catamount was intrigued. Nobody had ever approached him without a gun before, and he didn't rightly know what t' make of Jack, whether t' make him into a friend or a meal, so he just came t' the mouth of the cave and growled, "Tell me why I shouldn't make you my next meal."

Tryin' t' get that big cat on his side an' t' NOT eat him, Jack said, "I know you're a real king here, one with true character, and not like the farmer who only got it b'cause o' his name. In fact, I think you're *true* name must really be 'Aslan' like in that book my teacher at school tol' us t' read – *The Lion, The Witch and The Wardrobe.*" I don't like t' read much, but that story was a good 'un, and the Lion, who is a real hero, his name is Aslan. So, I reckon your name must really be 'Aslan.' AND, I think you're kindly getting' tired of old Farmer King accusin' you of somethin' you didn't do and all o' his boastin about bein' so important. I had something like 'at and it really burned me up. People all th' time was writing stories about a boy named Jack and makin' him out t' be a trickster, a liar, or a thief. I ain't none of them, but b'cause his name was Jack in their stories, people – like Farmer King – think that's what I am, too. Mebbee you want t' help me and the other people in this here cove put Farmer King in his place."

The Catamount raised an eyebrow and said, "Tell me

why I can trust you. Give me a reason t' believe you're not one of them tricksters."

Jack looked at 'im square in the eye and said, "You have t' decide that y'rself. But ask yr'self, 'even if Jack's a trickster, wouldn't it be worth it jes' t' show ol' Farmer King for what he really is?' I ain't no trickster."

The Catamount said, "I'm in. What now?"

Jack studied on it a minute, then said, "I go t' all the cove folk t' explain our plan and get their support."

The Catamount was still puzzled. "What's th' plan?"

Jack replied, "Well, I reckon ol' King got his own livestock hid where nobody could find 'em. Catamount, I bet you been creepin' around this cove, goin' places nobody else done been." (Catamount nods.) Jack continues, "We got t' go get them critters b'fore dawn, hide 'em ourselves – but you GOT T' PROMISE you won't, shall we say, make 'em disappear early."

Catamount raises an eye whisker, then, "Agreed. It'll be worth it t' expose Farmer King."

Jack says, "Then, b'fore sundown tomorrow, we take those critters back t' King's farm with me ridin' on y'r back t' show that you ain't a varmint. All the cove folk'll be there, too – I'll tell 'em t' get there a hour before we come and just stand around at the gate. Ol' King's family'll get real nervous and wonder what's goin' on. Then, when you and me come t' the gate, they'll some of em' go b'fore us, some on the sides, some behind. You and me'll be protected. We got t' take caution – they was a ol' Jack tale with Jack as a trickster, where Jack ends up ridin' a lion, *without* the lion's permission, t' a king's palace, but the King's men done shot him. Now, not bein' that kind of Jack, I cain't let that happen. I promise. I ain't no trickster. You an' me, we'll be as safe as the cove folk can make it."

The Catamount, he said, "I'll go talk t' the livestock. I know where they been hid, and we got a understandin'. After chore time tomorrow mornin', you go convince the cove folk t' he'p out."

Jack said, "Done and double done. We'll meet up a hour b'fore supper at the ol' giant chestnut stump at the edge of King's farm. You bring the livestock and we'll commence the parade."

So after he done his chores in the morning, one by one Jack went t' see Mr. Justis, Maw Padgett, the Kuykendall clan, ol' Johnny Israel, Lacey an' Nehi Douthitt, Arrie Cogdill, 'Stormy' Cloud, and Doc Blevins. Ev'ry last one of them good cove folk said they'd be there, and every last one of 'em promised t' protect Jack, the Catamount, and all o' King's critters.

So, at a hour before sunset, Jack and Aslan's plan was executed perfectly. As predicted, when the King family saw all the cove folk gathered at the gate, they DID get nervous, and when the crowd didn't scatter, them boys went and got their guns. But with Mr. Justis, Maw Padgett's clan, the Kuykendalls, Johnny, Lacey, Arrie, Stormy, and Doc, them boys took nary a shot. Jack rode up on the back of Aslan, leadin' the missin' critters, hopped off and strolled right up t' Farmer King and said, "Farmer King, whatcha got t' say t' these good cove folk?"

Farmer King, he knew he'd been bested, and not by trickery nor lyin'. But he also saw, for the first time in years, the good folk of the cove. He simply said, "I done tol' Jack I'd give him a reward of $1000 if he brought my missin' livestock or the carcass o' what had took 'em. Well, he done both – I didn't say the carcass had t' be dead. So I reckon I owe $2000. And if Jack's half the person that all y'all are, I know he'll make good for the whole cove with the reward."

And that's exactly what he did. Jack put the reward money to real good use. First, he made certain-sure that the missin' King livestock got new homes with people who promised to take good care of 'em. Second, he arranged for each of the cove famlies to get a replacement for one critter they lost to a predator – a fox, bear, coyote, or even a owl last year. In exchange for Catamount's promise to protect all the farms in the cove, the cove folk promised to protect him as well. In addition, they said that 'Aslan,' as they were startin' to call him, could eat any outside predators he caught trying to pilfer cove livestock. Fin'ly, Jack done set up a farmer's market to sell produce from the cove and started a bizness to market and sell the wild 'sang that cove folk found on their land!

Because o' what happened in this here tale, the good folk of Brook's Cove were safe, happy, and prosperin'. Aslan was not seen for weeks at a time, but the cove critters all were safe. And Farmer King, well let's just say that unlike King Saul, who became un-annointed, he done got transformed into a right good man, and like it's wrote in Ezekiel, the Lord give him a new heart.

Jack and
the Garli-Cousins

Y'all ain't gonna b'lieve this,
but it's true, at least as true as a Jack Tale oughta be...

I seen it with my own eyes, heard it with my own ears, and smelled it with my own nose. Let's just say that I was in on the whole thing. Y' know, they say smell conjures up memories even more than other senses, and I have t' tell you, the memory of this, shall we say, sitch-u-ation is still very real.

Jack heard from Mr. Justis (who else knows the cove better'n him?) that that partic'lar year was predicted t' be especially good for the southern Appalachian prize known as ramps. Ramps is also known as a wild leek, or a kissin' cousin t' the wild onion or garlic (hence the name o' this tale). Throughout Appalachia, it's a celebrated seasonin', and now, why it's a delicacy in fancy restaurants in New York City and with high class "foodies" in other places. But just being kin and a delicacy don't mean it's gentle on the nose. In Appalachia, ramps is known as the "King o' Stink!" (A quick heads-up -- in the High Country, there ain't no such thing as a "ramp." "Ramps" is always both singular and plural – kind of like "y'all".)

Jack's Mama, Miss Dayle, was a real good cook, and used what was grown in gardens, "harvested" on the mountain, and plucked from the hidden sections of the cove. She knew how t' use ramps t' make soups and stews much tastier, but that was just the beginning. She grilled 'em, pickled 'em, and fried 'em; she cooked 'em with eggs and grits, with wild mountain trout, and with zucchini; she made 'em into sauces, dressings, and even savory jams. There was almost no end t' the recipes she created, but y' had t' move quick-like – ramp season is short, and in Jack's neck of the woods, it usually meant sometime in March. Ramps is a hardy plant – a Southern Appalachian winter, even in parts of the High Country, cain't deter it from bein' a whatchacall "harbinger" o' spring.

But I digress. Y'all signed on for a Jack Tale, and all I've done so far is give you some back story. I better get t' the 'Tale' part.

Word up in Brooks Cove was that the ramps was comin' on and ready t' be dug. But cove folk had an understandin' that nary a person could overdig the ramps, even if they found a large patch of 'em. So Jack knew he better not take more than a few. (Trust me, a few ramps goes a long way…) One Tuesday square in the middle of ramp season, Jack went out t' his special ramps patch and picked his quota for his mama Dayle before headin' off t' school. On his way t' school, Jack kindly wandered off the beaten track because he saw another small patch of ramps and thought he might get a special treat t' have mid-morning – y'know — between classes. So, he dug himself a couple of ramps and stuck 'em in his front left pocket t' keep for later. He didn't give no never mind t' the fact that ramps are, shall we say, "odiferous" — everyone he knew up in the cove, and most of his classmates at school grew up on ramps as a natural part of spring cookin.'

Comin' on t' third period, Jack was a little hurried and didn't have his snack b'fore class. He walked in almost late, but before he even set two steps inside the room, his teacher, Mr. James (I knew him very well, if you catch my drift…) he said," Jack, go out the door and pitch 'em down the bank."

"Pitch what?" replied Jack.

"Your ramps, Jack" said Mr. James, almost without lookin' at Jack.

"I ain't got no ramps," said Jack.

"I can smell 'em," said Mr. James. This time his eyes drilled Jack like a blue laser.

"I picked some for Mama before breakfast and left 'em with her b'fore comin' t' school – maybe that's what you smell."

"I picked my own quota before breakfast," said Mr. James. "What I smell is fresh, and the smell is comin' from your front left pocket."

Jack knew he'd been found out. Onliest thing left t' do

was t' try t' save his snack. "Please don't make me pitch 'em," pleaded Jack. "They're my snack – didn't you ever have school lunch here at school?"

"It wouldn't make a hen's bitty o' difference. Pitch em'," declared Mr. James, knowing it was just a matter of time now. *"And leave 'em lie."* Without saying a word, Jack stepped outside, ambled over t' the edge of the bank, took a look around, then pitched his ramps down that viney slope. He looked very carefully t' see where they landed. Then, with Mr. James' watchful eye, he came back t' the classroom.

Math class went awful slow, but Jack knew that after math come lunch and he'd have a chance t' retrieve his ramps from where he pitched 'em. Since they're so garlicky, don't no critters like 'em – way too hard on their noses. Wellsir, right at 11:43, the bell rang and Mr. James dismissed math class. But Jack could tell Mr. James was watching t' see what he would do. Jack went out the door and made like he was goin' t' the cafeteria. But as soon as he could, he got lost in the crowd of students, then found his way over t' the bank, scrambling down t' where the ramps had been pitched. He was so set on that snack that the thought of a school lunch left him as unsatisfied as a bear-stripped blueberry bush.

Just when Jack was getting close t' the ramps, his foot got caught in a vine and down he went. When he looked up t' see if he was being watched, he looked square in the face of a 6-foot-long king snake. Even Jack was surprised, but not scared – king snakes ain't vipers and they tend t' leave people alone -- and in a couple of shakes he learned that he wasn't half as scared as he should have been. Out of the blue, Jack heard Mr. James hollerin' at him t' not move. At first he thought it was because he'd been caught trying t' retrieve the ramps and Mr. James didn't want him t' get away. But there was somethin' in Mr. James' voice – and more importantly, somethin' in the eyes of that king snake that made him freeze. And in that moment, all Jack could see was a streak o'black shootin' over his leg and clampin' down on the jaw of a venomous copperhead who was ready t' strike through Jack's blue jeans. And in the next moment, he felt Mr. James's big hand clamp down on his arm and yank him away from the fightin' snakes.

The fight was over in a New York minute. Who won? Let's just say that King snakes aren't poisonous to humans, they're immune to vipers' venom, and they regularly eat copperheads. Him being big and all, that king snake had the advantage. "Ol' King," as Jack was beginnin' t' think of him, made his own snack out of that copperhead and seemed t' enjoy it as much as Jack would have enjoyed the ramps he'd brought for his pre-math snack.

* * *

In the process of the snakes fighting and Mr. James hauling Jack out the way, the ramps Jack pitched down that bank were destroyed. And as if that wasn't enough, Mr. James still had a hold on Jack's arm – but it wasn't a vice grip like it had been when he'd been pulled from the snake fight. Still, Jack expected a lecture on obedience, and he wasn't looking forward to it -- he had it comin'.

"Jack," came Mr. James' no-nonsense voice.

"Yessir." Jack was embarrassed about sneaking out, about falling, and about having t' be saved by Mr. James from the snakes.

"Are y' ok?" asked Mr. James. "Your ankle been sprained? Can y' stand up on your own?"

"Yessir," said Jack, only just now figuring out that Mr. James had been holding him up.

"Well I guess God sent two of us t' help you out."

"Two of y'all?" Jack was a little confused. "It was you who pulled me out of there."

Mr. James was a little surprised at Jack's confusion. "Yep. 'twas. But all I did was get you out the way; it wouldn't have been in time if it hadn't been for that king snake." Mr. James went on, "That king, he's the one who really saved you. If it'd been just me, we'd be on the way t' the hospital t' get 'de-venomized' by Doc Blevins. Everyone up around here knows he keeps some copperhead anti-venom ready for snake situations like this."

"Thank you, Mr. James. I 'preciate it," was all Jack could muster right then. Still a little confused, Jack went on, "Ain'tcha goin' t' lecture me?"

"What for?" asked Mr. James. "What do you need t' be lectured on?"

"Well, for starters, I brought those ramps into school. I knew better, but I love 'em so much, and I hate school lunches so bad, that I couldn't help myself," stated Jack.

"You have a point," replied Mr. James. "What else?"

"Then I snuck away at lunch t' fetch 'em back."

"I'd a done the self-same thing when I was your age," said Mr. James. "But I hope I'd have been a little more careful before rushing into a batch of vines. You and I both know that's a snake's paradise."

"I know, Mr. James," Jack answered back, "but I couldn't help myself."

"Well, I guess this might have just a little bit of a lecture in it after all," said Mr. James. "Fact is, Jack, you could have helped yourself. You just fell t' temptation, thinking about how much you wanted the ramps. Wantin' 'em is not the problem. Ignoring the fact that you'd been told t' *leave 'em lie* was your problem. I know you remember that God won't allow ary temptation that's stronger than His Spirit can strengthen you against. And you also remember what Paul said t' Timothy – God gave us a spirit of power and love and self-control. But rememberin' what was written and actin' on it are very different things."

"Yessir."

"Well, lunch time is near over. We need t' be getting back up the bank for 4th period," said Mr. James. "Lecture is over, but you gotta promise me 2 things – no, three."

"Yessir."

"First, you promise me you won't go traipsing through viney areas without something t' defend yourself against vipers."

"Yessir. Maybe I could get my own king snake t' take with me when I have t' go through a bunch of vines," said Jack. Mr. James just looked at him so that Jack knew it was a dumb thing to say.

"Second, promise me y'all will start meditatin' and buildin' up your self-control," said Mr. James.

"I'll try," replied Jack.

"Try?" stated Mr. James. "Ain't no room for 'try' in the life of a cove boy."

"Yessir. I'll study and act on self-control. And the third thing?" asked Jack.

Mr. James just smiled. "You get your Mama t' make me some of her savory ramp jam. I'll even bring her a batch of ramps from my own secret patch."

"I'll do it," said Jack.

And as far as anyone up around Brooks Cove knows, Jack told nary a person about what really happened at school that day, him nearly gettin' bit by a copperhead, but they did think it was a mite interestin' that Jack started workin' more on his math and that a new Tale popped up on the storytellin' circuit about it takin' a King and a Teacher to save a boy from a viper...

Jack and
the Parkway Fog

Y'all ain't gonna b'lieve this,
but it's true, at least as true as a Jack Tale oughtta be...

Jack told me about it just after him and Mr. Cogdill (one
o' Jack's neighbors who lived up in Brooks Cove) got back
from their *specialty* produce run. I been in Parkway fogs
many a time, and I can tell you certain sure – they's not
much t' see. One thing I know f' sure is that Carl Sandburg

got it wrong in a big way! They ain't no such thing as a *Parkway* fog "comin' in on little cat feet!" Maybe *Chicago* fogs do that, but *Parkway* fogs don't mess around. They come stompin' in on feet that'd make ol' Aslan's (*the cove's adopted Catamount*) feet look tiny! Sandburg shoulda known better, him livin' in Flatrock and all. Why that's no more'n 15 mile or so from the Parkway.

But I done promised you a tale about Jack, not just about fogs. Well, here it goes. Jack's Mama, Miss Dayle, was up to her elbows tryin' t' get her cookin' done for the upcomin' week, but she didn't have enough green beans. So she sent Jack down to the Brooks Cove Farmer's Market t' get some o' Arrie Cogdill's half runners. Seems like Jack was always hungry, bein' a growin' boy and all, and he couldn't think o' nothin' more important than helpin' his Mama put food on the table. So off he took t' the farmer's market t' find Mr. Cogdill.

When Jack got down t' the market, he was disappointed t' see that Mr. Cogdill's booth was nigh on t' empty. "Mr. Cogdill!" cried Jack. "If I don't get Mama her half runners, our dinner Thursday won't be near so good! Cain'tcha help a growin' boy out?"

"I know your story, boy," replied Arrie, "and it ain't half so bad as you're makin' it out t' be. Tell y' what. I still got a peck o' them beans at home, and I'll give 'em t' Miss Dayle…" Mr. Cogdill paused for effect, "**IF** you he'p me out with my run up t' the Cloudland Inn."

"Why're y' goin' up there, Mr. Cogdill?" asked Jack.

"Got t' take my *specialty* produce up there," answered Arrie. "A couple o' months ago, the new fertilize I put out on my garden kicked in and within a week I knew I was gonna have more'n I could sell in our Brooks Cove Farmer's Market. So, I started lookin' around t' see could I find another outlet AND I planted some whatchacall *specialty* produce just t' see what it'd be like. I'd heard about Cloudland makin' a comeback, so I called 'em up and they was delighted – said their new chef was lookin' for all he could get – o' *specialty* produce. Playin' with 'em t' see how smart they was, I tol' 'em the ramps was gone back in March. They said they was lookin' for fresh eggplant, kohlrabi, Jerusalem artichoke -- things like 'at. I tol' 'em I grow those vegetables. But, I told 'em I might could sell 'em t' Cloudland if the deal was good -- they'd have t' guarantee me they'd for sure buy my whole crop o' specialty vegetables. I let 'em stew on it for a while (get it--'stew on it'?! Y'uns are s'posed t' laugh at that pun!) Anyways, they agreed to my terms. So today I got t' get my specialty produce up t' Cloudland. Are ya in? Wanna get them beans for your Mama? I already got the truck loaded."

"Y' got a deal, Mr. Cogdill. I'll go tell Mama she'll get her beans. Can you pick me up on your way out the cove?"

"I'll see you then. I know your Mama is cookin' right now, so I'll bring them half runners when I pick you up. And," said Arrie, "I got a surprise for y', too."

After droppin' off the beans, Jack and Mr. Cogdill took off out the cove. Up till about 15 year ago, Arrie hadn't never been outside the county, and mostly he stayed up in the Cove, so havin' a truck and drivin' somewhere more'n 20 miles away was a big deal. Trouble was, tho', that on this August mornin', after leavin' the cove they got onto the Blue Ridge Parkway and straight away they was in a *Parkway* fog. Now to those o' you who ain't been in one, y' gotta understand – when y'r in a *Parkway* fog, y' cain't see nary a thing more'n 10 feet away. Jack was gettin' all white-knuckled, knowin' they was gonna be on the

Doug Jones

Parkway for the next 13 miles. T' try t' calm Jack down, Arrie asked, "Jack, d'you know what the folk over in Mabel say about countin' August fogs?"

"I got no idee, Mr. Cogdill," said Jack.

"Wellsir," continued Arrie, "they say that if you count the number of fogs in August, it'll tell y' how many heavy snowfalls they'll be in the winter."

"Is 'at true, Mr. Cogdill?" asked Jack. "Some o' them kinds o' predictin' seems pretty farfetched t' me."

"I don't rightly know," said Arrie, with a twinkle in his eye. "Some of 'em, like predictin' the hardness of a winter by the fall *mast* makes sense t' me. Critters got t'eat, y'know. Others, like those with woolly-bear caterpillars, don't. Why, one time your teacher Mr. James told me that he saw two woolly bears crawl out from under the self-same leaf pile at the self-same time on the self-same day. One of 'em was mostly light brown, the other was mostly black as a cove night. Mr. James, he said, 'how could the woolly bear be any good at predictin' if two of 'em like 'at couldn't get it right between themselves?' Then again, maybe they's somethin' to th' fogs."

Arrie kep' on, tellin' Jack some stories from when he was comin' on. "They was this one time when me an' m' kin were gonna go pick blueberries up in the crags on the other side o' Brooks Cove. It was about the end o' July, and since we couldn't jus' walk there and get back in a day, we had t' wait till Cousin Tom could get his daddy's truck for a day. That day came in the first week o' August. Boy was we ready – couldn't hardly get over t' the crags without droolin, thinkin' about them blueberries. And Tom said he'd seen 'em one year when the bushes were nigh onto 8 feet tall!"

Jack was startin' t' drool himself. "Whadja do, Mr. Cogdill?"

"Well, we came round the last curve b'fore we was gonna park the truck, and our hearts dropped! Nary a blueberry on all them bushes! We seen another truck on the side o' the road, and a boy said, 'bears.' I said back t' him, 'o' course they's bears up here. Where else 'r they gonna go?' That boy said right back at me, 'They done got 'em all – all the blueberries. Aubrey my cousin said they got 'em last week."

Jack said, "The nerve o' them bears. I'll tell y' what I'd a done. I'd a gone that week earlier. I'd a grabbed all my dirty white socks, stuffed 'em in m' pockets, grabbed Angelo, and we'd a showed 'em whose blueberries they was. Course, in Cove fashion, I'd a left some berries on the bushes – y' know, for the bears t'glean."

Arrie nodded his head as Jack was finishin' up. "Ya got a point, Jack," said Arrie. "But they's another reason I wanted t'have you come with me today. Lookin' at the weather up in the cove early this mornin', I reckoned it was gonna be a day for a Parkway fog. When I saw you this mornin' comin in for them beans, I thought, 'Arrie, you need t' tell that boy Jack about his Papaw and his experience with such a fog. He's growin' up enough t' hear 'bout it, and it'll be kindly a surprise t' him, too.' Y'know, Jack, you was named for your Papaw – his name was Jack, too. He was a good man, but he hadn't always been like 'at."

Now, as the narrator o' this here tale, and since I now got two different Jack's in this self-same tale, I gotta make sure you can tell them Jacks apart. We'll call the Jack o' my stories – y'know, "Jack and the Bear Scarin' Socks," "Jack and the Cave Eyes," and the others – we'll call him just "Jack." And the Jack that was his Papaw – we'll call him Jack th'Elder. First thing you listeners need to know is that

Jack th'Elder passed on a while ago and Jack didn't get t'have much time with him. So Arrie Cogdill, who *did* get t' know him well, Arrie wanted t' pass on a little o' Jack th'Elder's wisdom that come from his experiences – like bein' in a Parkway fog.

"By the time he was a teenager," Arrie continued, "Jack th'Elder had tricked a few people and stolen a few things, like the Jack in the traditional Jack Tales. But he never thought it'd hurt nobody. He done took a piece of bubblegum here, a loaf o'bread there. One time he convinced a family over in Lester Cove – in the next county over – that they could get their bees t' make the lightest locust flower honey that'd last 18 years without sugarin' if they'd let Jack th'Elder take it over t' Clays Cove where he lived and he could keep a eye on it for 'em. What he didn't tell 'em was that it was a trick --he was doin' it just t' be able t' rob the hive whenever he wanted. Why, Jack th'Elder even "borrowed" a truck one night from some farmer across the ridge where they wadn't no road t' connect t' his own cove just t' see if he could do it. Kep' it most o' the night, and when he took it back, the farmer was madder'n a bunch o' ground hornets and just as ready t' sting. Jack th'Elder weaseled himself out of it by sayin' he'd brought the truck back full o' gas. What he *didn't* say was that he'd got the gas on a--shall we say--'five-finger-discount.'"

"But after a while, takin' advantage of good folk in neighborin' coves took its toll on Jack th'Elder. He got t' the point that he had a knot in his stomach near all th' time, and he began t' make it up t' the folk he took from or tricked – even up to 4 times what he cheated 'em, just like in the Bible. But even after he turned from his thievin' and trickster ways, he still was accused of doin' wrong. The sheriff, who'd a been watchin' through all this, started t' shall we say "benefit" himself and the men on his payroll and blame it on Jack th'Elder."

"Try as he might, with the sheriff out t' get him, Jack th'Elder couldn't escape his past. Seemed like ever' time he set out t' make things right, the sheriff done made up new – and false – charges against him. The sheriff done accused Jack th'Elder of thievery and of getting-gain by tricking good folk out of their money or their property. It was bad. Jack th'Elder had been sure for a long time that it was the sheriff and the men on his payroll who was doin' the theivin' and the trickin', but the sheriff was a powerful man, and Jack th'Elder was in despair."

"It got so bad that Jack th'Elder thought escapin' the charges was hopeless and was almost ready to give up t' the sheriff. But just as the deputies was comin' t' get him for some tricksterin' they'd been doin' themselves, somethin' tol' Jack th'Elder t' go up toward the ridge. When he was only about a quarter mile from the ridgeline, his heart sank -- a thick fog started to roll in. Jack th'Elder had seen clouds on the mountain before, but he hadn't never been up near the ridge when it was in the clouds. He didn't know whether it was meant t' help him or confuse him, but the same voice that tol' him t' go toward the ridge tol' him t' continue. That fog, why it was so thick he couldn't see more'n a arm's length in front of his face. Jack th'Elder, he had no idea what t' do. His mind was racin' s' fast, thinkin' about the sheriff and his men, that he couldn't hear whether the voice was tellin' him t' continue or t' stop. He didn't have no light, no compass, no landmarks – nothing t' depend on. And it had got so dark in the fog, he couldn't tell whether it was day or night. So he hunkered down t' wait it out. All's he could do was wait. And pray. And the prayin' stilled Jack th'Elder's mind to where he could remember what someone once tol' him: 'When you fix your mind on giants, you stumble. When you fix your mind on God, the giants tumble.' He didn't understand it when he was tol', and he wadn't sure he understood it in the fog. But he didn't have nothing else he could count on. So, he fixed his mind on God the best he could."

"In a few minutes (*that seemed like forever!*), a small clearing opened up. It was like a hallway about 10 feet long and 4 feet wide – small, but enough. Jack th'Elder felt a supernatural callin' t' follow it – couldn't be no worse than doin' nothin'. He took a few steps and the clearing moved downward a few steps with 'im. He did it again, and the fog parted again, just enough t' show him he was bein' took care of. In about a quarter mile, a few steps at a time, it got unusually light – the fog lifted. Jack th'Elder knew the fog itself delivered him from his enemy just like God delivered His people from their enemies a whole mess o' times. Jack th'Elder was finally safe, the sheriff was lost in the fog, and Jack th'Elder knew that things was gonna be ok.

Turns out that the sheriff's men, who also done got lost in the fog, found their way outta the fog after several hours, bein' run around that ridgetop like th' Israelites in the desert. They was so a-feared they headed right t' Judge Buckner and admitted their own thievery and trickery t' get a lighter sentence. The judge sent out a party t' find and bring in the sheriff. He was later charged with theivin' and bein' a trickster in several coves. Needless t' say, he wadn't elected sheriff again."

* * *

"It was a real turn-around," said Arrie. "Through hard work and smart farmin', Jack th'Elder fin'ly started t' get ahead a little. After a few years he had raised enough money and good will t' stake a claim on a place up in Brooks Cove t' make his way. He courted and married a local gal named Eulagene –she's y'r Mamaw— worked his own place AND he'ped out on Eulagene's daddy's place just b/cause it was the right thing t' do. Jack th'Elder was finally seen by the people of Trail County as not bein' a trickster nor a thief and was determined that his legacy would be that his children and their children and their children would never again be seen as tricksters nor thieves."

Arrie started t' wrap it up. "I knowed it would be hard fer you t' understand without bein' in a *real* Parkway fog. It was for me when I was comin' on. But I checked with Miss Eulagene jus' t' be sure o' the details. You know y'r MaMaw – she don't tell nary a word that ain't true."

"Your right about that, Mr. Cogdill," said Jack. "And I'm grateful for the story and the lesson. Powerful grateful. An' look – m'knuckles ain't white no more. I'm grateful for your safe drivin' in this fog, and for learnin' about my Papaw."

"Your welcome, Jack," finished Mr. Cogdill just as they were fixin' t' leave the Parkway. Sure enough, t'wadn't no more'n a quarter mile after they got off the Parkway, that the fog lifted. They went on t' Cloudland, Arrie sold his produce to the fancy hotel, and they headed on home t' Brooks Cove.

Jack and
the Post Turtle

Y'all ain't gonna b'lieve this,
but it's true – at least as true as a Jack Tale oughtta be...

Although I wadn't around when this situation come up, I'd seen it many a time over the years up in Brooks Cove or 'nother cove. Lacey Douthitt, Jack's neighbor, told me about it - said she thought it made a big impression on 'im. And Lacey oughtta know. It was her Papaw (her daddy's daddy), Isaiah Akers, that give the name Turtle Post Rd to an ol' loggin' road up 'bout half way up the mountain on th' left just past Jack's fam'ly home. It ain't traveled much now, 'cause the forest pretty well come back, but the tracks are clear and they's still some fence posts from when Mr. Isaiah marked off some o' his land. Lacey tol' me years ago about a time when Jack's Papaw, Jack th'Elder, was visitin' the cove an' playin' a prank on her Papaw.

Jack th'Elder found a box turtle and took it up t' the loggin' road, set it on top of a fence post and went and hid himself till Mr. Isaiah come by. (*For those o' you who've been payin' attention, despite his name, Isaiah was older than Jack th'Elder. So in good Southern tradition, Jack th'Elder called him "Mr. Akers," and I call him Mr. Isaiah.*) When he come up the road from his place, Mr. Isaiah looked at the turtle on the fence post, stopped t' consider it for a while, then asked, "What'cha doin' up here, Mr. Turtle?"

To his great surprise, the turtle said, "Didn't get here by m'self."

Without thinkin' it were odd for a turtle t' speak, Isaiah said, "Well, o' course you didn't. Nary a turtle has clumb a fence post by hisself. Are y' o.k.? Need some he'p?"

The turtle, a little annoyed and not thinkin' it odd that a human would talk t' a turtle, shot back, "Well, iff'n I couldn't get up here by m'self, y' think I could get down by m'self?"

Isaiah said, "Possibly, you havin' a hard shell an' all. You could tip y'self over and land in the grass and not be hurt a'tall. But I wadn't tryin' t' be a smart aleck; I was offerin' t' he'p you -- iff'n you want it."

With a change o' heart, the turtle said, "I'd be powerful obliged if y' could set me down pointed toward the creek.

I was on my way when that feller Jack th'Elder hijacked me and set me on the post."

Isaiah said, "I'd be right proud t' he'p you out, Mr. Turtle," then set him down pointed toward the creek. "I reckon that Jack fella was prankin' me just t' see what I'd do. I know he'll be around here somewhere. I need t' have a talk with 'im."

Mr. Isaiah spotted Jack th'Elder out the corner o' his eye, and without givin' anything away, snuck around all quiet like till he was right behind Jack. Jack th'Elder didn't know he was there.

"Jack," said Mr. Isaiah. It was a statement, not a question nor a scare, but Jack th'Elder near jumped outta his britches.

"Mr. Akers?! You done scared me."

"I meant to, Jack," said Isaiah. "I just had a little talk with our friend the post turtle. Seems like you kindly stopped his trek t' th' creek. He's a turtle, Jack—he needs water. He's o.k. now – you saw me set him on his way. Jack, you know the sayin', 'Iff'n you see a turtle on a fence post, you know he didn't get there by hisself.' Most everyone up here in the cove knows it, too. Truth be tol', it warn't much of a prank – and it turned out t' be harmless, too. What I want you t' know, though is that there may come a time when you can use it as a kind of a code when you need some help – you know, t' let someone know someone's been there not too long ago. But don't you never shame that code. Don't never use it just t' have y'r fun at someone else's expense. And, when you get back home t' Clays County, most of all, don't you neglect t' tell y'r family t' do the same."

"Yessir."

"Are we clear, Jack? Just t' be sure, I'm namin' this

loggin' road 'Turtle Post Rd." and putting a sign up with the name on it. Remember it." And for emphasis, "Remember."

"Yessir, Mr. Akers. I promise." And Jack th'Elder done kep' his word.

Well, that there's the back story for what Lacey was tellin' me about a few years ago. Then t'other day, she had a follow up. Seem like *our* Jack hadn't quite understood the wisdom of the post turtle.

Last Saturday a week, Jack was out walkin' up the mountain. He saw a box turtle along the side, and without thinkin' – just like Jack th'Elder he put it up on a post. Now the Eastern box turtle has a lifespan up to 100 years if it's protected, and this particular box turtle happened t' be the self-same turtle that Jack th'Elder had put on that self-same post, playin' a trick on ol' Mr. Isaiah. Later that day, Jack was plagued by the thought that he'd heard his Mamaw Eulajean tell of a turtle talkin' to Isaiah. Try as he might t' ignore it, he had second thoughts about havin' put that turtle on the post. Late that night, when he couldn't stand it no more, Jack went out to retrieve that turtle. He walked up t' Turtle Post Rd., but the turtle wadn't there. He began t' panic, but lookin' around for a spell, he finally saw the turtle layin in the grass a stone's throw away. Grateful, he picked the turtle up and took it over toward the creek t' be sure it'd get home.

The next mornin' at dawn, Jack went back to the fence post where the turtle had been. In the light o'day, he could see there had been a big ruckus there – signs of the Catamount was there, but they was also a bunch of vulture feathers scattered around. Sure as summer kudzu there had been some kind of a shall-we-say conflict, but he didn't know quite what it was. About that time, ol' Aslan came walkin' up to Jack. He said he'd been out on patrol last night and saw a vulture flying around, and he didn't like them unclean birds a'tall. Aslan had seen that turtle on the post and that vulture flyin' around and knowed somethin' was up.

"But," Aslan tol' Jack, "as for takin' care o' outside predators, they wadn't much I could do. Them vultures are as wiley as ol' Diablo the coyote and don't get low enough for me t' catch 'em. BUT, I know an eagle who occasionally comes near the cove; I called on him t' help chase the varmint away."

But it was a little late. That vulture had all a sudden swooped down, grabbed Jack's box turtle, and was climbin' up t' drop him down onto the rocks, hopin' his shell would crack or break. Y' see, a vulture ain't just an opportunist; when they ain't no carrion – and Aslan was doin' a good job of seein' the outside predators was out o' luck – a vulture'll turn into a bird of prey, which is what he done with Jack's box turtle. Anywho, that vulture done saw likely rocks and dropped that turtle. Luckily, Aslan's eagle friend was close by. He understood the danger and was able fly under the turtle, catch him, and bear 'im up on his wings. He quickly set the turtle safe on the ground close t' where Jack found him that mornin,' but immediately took off again. Aslan said he heard the eagle mutterin' "that vulture's worse 'n a fool's tongue! He needs t' get outta our neck of the woods."

So, the turtle was safe, but it wadn't straightforward. Jack headed back home t' get ready for church. After the service, Miss Lacey come up to him and said, "Jack – a word w' you. Y'all know the ol' loggin' road between our places that Papaw called Turtle Post Road." It was a 'rhetorical' question. (As one o' my young'uns pointed out when she was 7-year old, "That means they don't want ary answer.")

"Yes'm." Jack started to feel a little uncomfortable.

"I was outside last night and saw Aslan and an eagle into something. They was a ruckus goin' on for a while, then the eagle took off in hot pursuit of somethin.' When it settled down, I went and talked t' Aslan, and he told me about what happened with the turtle. We went over and found 'im in need of rest, but the markings on that turtle tol' me it was the same turtle my Papaw found all those years ago. I know the story about my Papaw Isaiah and your Papaw Jack th'Elder and the promise Jack th'Elder made t' not shame the turtle-on-a-fence post code. Eulajean tol' me your Papaw kep' his word. Sounds like mebbe you ain't done y'r part."

Jack replied, not quite getting the point. "But I went t' rescue the turtle. Had t' look around in the pitch black till I found him, then took him over toward the creek. I only found out this mornin' about what Aslan and the eagle done t' help out. Honest, Miss Lacey, I was tryin' t' do somethin' good!"

"That ain't the point, Jack" said Miss Lacey. "The post turtle in Papaw's story could blame Jack th'Elder fer his predicament. Bein' put up on that fence post weren't *none* o' his doin'. But he was a turtle – not a person. But you, son, while you might not be completely responsible for all the *sitch-u-ayshuns* you find y'self in, you ain't completely innocent, neither."

"You ain't talkin' 'bout the turtle now, are y'?" asked Jack.

"Nossir Jack," Said Miss Lacey. "Thanks to Aslan, the eagle, and you, that turtle is fine again. But, I want you t' think about somethin' else – somethin' related that I'm certain sure you never done thought of. What if those times you was in trouble – all y'r 'sitch-u-ayshuns' as you call 'em—what if nary one of'm was y'r doing. A*nd*, what if what happened today was not your fault, not anyone else's fault. What if it was simply the Lord allowing some trouble in order t' work on your character?"

"I know y'r tales, Jack," continued Miss Lacey. "Remember how Angelo saved you from the bear? You weren't doin' nothin' that wouldn't have been o.k. here in the cove – young 'uns always spend a fair amount of time by themselves out-o'-doors. But you probably shouldn't have gone off by y'rself. Fortunate for you that Angelo had a job t' do and he put his whole heart into it."

Jack, droppin' his eyes, "Yes'm."

"And remember how Mr. James saved you from the snake fight? And how you got him t' give y' a lecture? Y' already allowed as how y' shouldn't of disobeyed and tried t' retrieve them ramps. The lecture wadn't about obedience nor respect. It was about self-control. *And*, you put the rescuers in danger, too."

Jack, truly humbled by now, "Yes'm. I wadn't thinkin. I guess that's a big problem for me – doin' before thinkin'. My character's pretty sorry."

"Don't you go givin' y'rself a pity party, Jack. Remember," said Miss Lacey. She added for emphasis, "Remember that you sometimes find y'rself in trouble. Remember that others done bailed you out many a time. You need t' make some changes, son, and be transformed by what you remember so that you don't get into trouble near so much. Rememberin' is Biblical."

"Yes'm, Miss Lacey," said Jack. "And thank you for takin' the time t' check on the turtle, talk with Aslan, and have the courage t' correct me. I appreciate it. And I promise to remember." Then workin' up his courage t' talk w' Miss Lacey like the friend she was t' ever'one in the cove, "Miss Lacey, can I ask you another question?"

"O'course, Jack, I'm y'r neighbor," said Miss Lacey. "What's on y'r mind?"

"I just wanted t' know how y'r husband Nehi got his name," said Jack.

Miss Lacey just laughed. "Did you think it was 'cause he likes a grape Nehi?"

Jack said, "Will and me was just wonderin.'"

"Well, the real reason is that folk 'round these parts have known 'im and done watched 'im grow up since he was 'knee high t' a grasshopper," said Miss Lacey. "He just figgered it was easier to spell it 'Nehi' than 'Knee-high.' Plus, he thought it'd be fun."

"Thank you, Miss Lacey. Fer ever'thing." Jack give her a big hug.

"Y'r welcome, Jack," smiled Miss Lacey. And with a twinkle in her eye, she said, "Remember."

Jack the Captivator

Y'all ain't gonna b'lieve this,
but it's true, at least as true as a Jack Tale oughtta be...

Jack told me about it just a few days after Stormy helped him take care of an owl Jack found in a meadow up the mountain a ways. Everbody in Brooks Cove knows that Stormy is a man of few words. When he speaks, you better listen even if you don't want to; his words 'r important. That's what finally bent Jack's ear and made 'im a little more thoughtful than he woulda been if left to himself.

Like most every week when he wadn't busy with school or working for somebody in the Cove, Jack was out roamin' the Blue Ridge. While he sauntered across a meadow leading up t' the High Country – kind of like a bald—Jack's attention was drawn to a murder of crows a-making a ruckus he had heard before. *(Murder?! It might not mean what you think up on the bald.)* Jack done heard that ruckus before, and he was certain-sure those crows was pesterin' some other critter, likely a great horned owl. Ever since Jack was a young'un, the wisdom o' the Cove held that havin' owls around was a good thing – as good as having king snakes like in Jack's ad-venture with the ramps—but that crows are raucus pests. *(You ever stop to think that "raucus" and "ruckus" sound a lot alike? Like whatever is raucus is likely to "raise a ruckus?" Amazin' what'll sidetrack you when you're tellin' a story.)*

Wellsir, Jack headed over to see could he break up the mess the crows were making, and when they saw him coming, they cleared out. Jack found a Great Horned Owl that had been pestered and pecked nearly t' death and was in a state of shock because of the crows. He didn't know if the owl would make it, but knowing the crows would come back to the owl quicker'n a duck on a June bug, Jack decided it was better for him t' risk carrying the owl with him and see if he could help it back t' health. Problem was, as Jack came t' find out when it came out of shock, that owl wasn't going t' agree that Jack was being **kind** by trying t' help.

Now Jack had toted a lunch with him when he set out, and still had the burlap bag it was in. So after he picked up the owl while it was in shock, he quickly put the bag over its head and closed it up so the owl wouldn't try t' fly away. By the time he was getting back t' Brooks Cove, the owl was coming to itself and wasn't going to, shall we say, "cooperate." Not knowing what t' do, but knowing that owl was still in danger, Jack took the strip of leather he'd tied up his lunch bag with and used it t' bind the owl's feet and then closed the bag around him. He knew he was going have t' get someone who knew about owls – or birds or critters – to look at his owl to see was it all right.

Didja catch that? Jack was thinkin "his" owl. The owl certain-sure didn't think of itself as <u>belongin'</u> *t' Jack. Trouble's a brewin'.*

Anyway, since Jack knew that Doc Blevins was out o' the county, he thought the next best person t' look at his owl was Stormy Cloud, so he headed up toward Stormy's place, just one homestead below Doc's. When he was coming t' the gate, Stormy, who was tendin' his herb patch, saw Jack and came t' meet him, thinkin' to himself, "What's in the bag?"

"Mr. Cloud, I need your help – at least my owl here needs your help," cried Jack.

"Hey, Jack."

"It's a Great Horned Owl," said Jack. "He was minding his own business, prob'ly just passing' time till dusk, or maybe he was half asleep, when all a sudden he got mobbed by a flock o' crows. They were worse than just being pests, they were trying t' kill him! I was out in the hills and heard their ruckus from across a bald, so I went t' see what they were up to. Lord knows I don't want t' lose no owls up here."

"I don't blame you none, Jack," said Stormy. "Crows can be right mean when they're trying to protect their hatchlings. As much as I like having owls around, and as much as I hate t' say it, the owl might not have been innocent – he's a raptor, Jack, always on the lookout for prey. Let's have us a look."

Jack held the bag while Stormy carefully opened it. The owl was not in good shape and had worn itself out even more by fightin' the bag while Jack was walking up to Stormy's place. "He's in bad shape, Jack. You need t' get him to a protected area and get him some food t' eat to help him get stronger. IF you can do that, he ought to be o.k. again by Monday a week. But don't try t' get too close, God didn't make him t' be your pet."

"Yessir. I'll do it," said Jack as he started back down t' his home place. And over his shoulder he called out t' Stormy, "We've got space in our winter barn where he'll be safe."

During the next week, Jack kep' his eye on the owl and made sure he had enough voles and an occasional rabbit, and that there was water for him to drink. But he didn't do so well with not thinking of him as a pet or a trained hunter – kind of like the "falconers" he read about from Scotland or England. He imagined himself as King Jack the Falconer with his own owl who would hunt on command and bring prey back for the King's feasts.

Now fer sure trouble ain't far away ….

Monday a week came and Jack could see that the owl, who he was calling Joshua because owls are great warriors, was ready to get back t' his own territory. So, Jack got dressed up in his heavy coveralls, put on his thick fireplace gloves, and covered his face t' protect himself. Then he untied the owl, intendin' t' let it fly around in the winter barn. Boy, was he in for a surprise! That owl took off like a silent bolt of caged lightning and then swooped down t' attack Jack. Jack scrambled, trying t' get somewhere the owl couldn't sink his talons into him. He finally crawled between a wall and a bunch of boards he was supposed to stack last week. After a few swoops, 'Joshua' got wore out again and Jack was able t' get out the door and close it up tight so the owl couldn't get out. That was close!

After he caught his breath, Jack took off t' see if he could find Stormy and get his help again. He still wanted t' help the owl, even if it had been tryin' t' attack him there in the winter barn. On his way up the cove road t' Stormy's place, Lacey Douthitt saw Jack and hollered to him, "Jack – what's y'r hurry?"

Over his shoulder, Jack hollered back, "I gotta find Mr. Cloud, Miss Lacey. Sorry I ain't got time t' come talk with y'."

"Well, I saw him earlier this morning – he's at home. Hope y' find him quick. Are y' in some kind of trouble?"

"I promise I'll come back and tell y' later, Ma'am."

When Jack came a-runnin' into his yard, Stormy saw him from his porch and had a good idea there must be something wrong with the owl.

"Mr. Cloud, you gotta come help me with the owl. He nearly attacked me."

"Catch your breath, son. Tell me about it."

Jack relayed the story about gettin' food and water for the owl, and said he reckoned that since today was Monday a week – the very day Stormy predicted the owl might be OK t' be on his own again – Jack thought he'd see how Joshua would do flying around in the winter barn.

Stormy just listened. "And..."

"So when I untied his legs and took the hood off his head, he swooped around a couple of times and then came like fury t' attack me. I'd got all dressed up t' pr'tect m'self from his talons if he should try t' land on my arm, but I never thought he was gonna try t' *attack* me. I was just trying t' *help* him recover from those blamed crows."

"Where is he now, Jack?"

"He's still in the barn – with the doors shut. I think he's

OK in there, but I don't know what t' do with him. I need your help."

"Come walk with me a spell, Jack. That owl will be fine where he is. He'll get tired and calm down. After a while when we get down to the barn, we'll tend to him. But then we'll have t' set him free."

"Set him free?! Mr. Cloud, even though he tried t' attack me, I still want to …"

"What? Keep him?" asked Stormy. "Make him a pet?! Ain't nothin' good can come of that!"

Jack came up short. He remembered Stormy's original advice, *"God didn't make him to be your pet."*

"Yessir." Jack dropped his eyes. "I was thinkin' what it'd be like t' keep him. I'm sorry, Mr. Cloud, I know you tried t' tell me he wasn't gonna be no pet, but I guess I just wanted t' think maybe he would be."

"We'll have t' let him go, Jack. And, you need t' know why it's personal to me."

"You know I got Cherokee blood, don't you?"

"Yessir. That's why I came t' you for help. You always seem t' know about critters and such. Plus, your name and all."

"There's more to it than that, Jack, but I appreciate that you thought you could come to me, and I'm grateful for your friendship. Not everyone outside this cove thinks of the Cherokee like that. Do you remember hearing about the 'Trail of Tears'?"

"When the government rounded up all the Cherokee and forced them walk all the way to Oklahoma? Yessir, we learned about it in school. I thought it was so mean, especially since you've always been part of our cove."

"One of my ancestors, about 5 great's ago, was forced to go on that trail. His name was High Cloud, and I'm proud to have his same last name. That part of my family history is nigh onto sacred to us and has been passed down from generation to generation. High Cloud endured the Trail and was one of the 'fortunate' ones who made it there. He said the worst part of it all was that when the government took him, he felt like he was losin' everything – his land, his heritage, his dignity – and all he wanted to do was to lash out like a weasel in a trap. He quickly learned there wadn't no point in that – all's he would do was hurt himself more. So he kept on the trail till they got to 'Indian Land' in Oklahoma."

"It was a terrible hard life, but whilst he was just barely hangin' on, he had a whatchcall "epiphany" – they was one thing they couldn't take from him – his thoughts. As long as he could think, as long as High Cloud could maintain his memories and his vision, he could regain and retain his dignity. High Cloud survived and helped others to regain their dignity. A few of 'em were able to return to their ancient homeland in Appalachia; some of 'em—not all— stayed, some of 'em thrived, and some, like me, have remained. High Cloud passed on the lessons he learned to his family and friends, and through the years of being mistreated and misjudged, they held on to the fact that they didn't need to be nobody's captive so long as they could take their own thoughts captive."

"And that's a good lesson for you right about now, Jack. The only thing it's right for a fella like you to take captive is your thoughts. When they's good thoughts, make 'em serve yourself and others. It's never wrong to try to help someone else become wiser and more respectful. When they's bad thoughts, force 'em to be quiet and not lead you or others down a bad road. It's hard. And the struggle will never go away, but it'll get easier when you practice it. Sometimes when I'm beginnin' t' think bad thoughts, I just tell myself, 'Be still.' And sometimes I pray that God will confuse them thoughts so that they don't all come together and gang up on me till I give in."

"Mr. Cloud – I can't believe you *ever* have bad thoughts. I ain't never even seen you angry!" Jack was truly astonished.

"We all get bad thoughts at times, Jack. I'm no exception. No one is. But followin' my advice at least gives you a fightin' chance." Stormy wanted to finish the 'lesson.' "Back to the owl."

"In my Cherokee heritage, owls are respected as extraordinary hunters. They're beautiful birds, they show courage, and people even think they are wise." Stormy paused, his eyes twinkling, "But I don't know how wise it is t' hunt skunks."

Jack laughed. Everyone in the cove knows that owls hunt skunks, and they're glad the owls keep the skunk population under control.

"Let's go take care of the owl, Jack. And set him free."

"Thank you, Mr. Cloud. Thank you for your story about High Cloud and your advice about bein' still. I promise t' not try t' turn him – or other critters -- into a pet."

It's a hard road, trying to take your thoughts captive. Jack and Stormy got the owl taken care of, and Jack did, indeed, go back to tell Lacey Douthitt about his incident. More important, Jack started tryin' to take his thoughts captive. Sometimes he was successful, sometimes not so much, but he kept a-workin' on it. After a while, Jack – and some of the others in the Cove – could see a difference. And so will you. Next time you're up in Brooks Cove, and I hope it's soon, your ears might perk up -- you might just hear Maw Padgett's young'uns or some of the Kuykendall clan hollerin' out t' each other, "Be Still!"

Jack and the
Turtle Post Waterfall

Y'all ain't gonna b'lieve this,
but it's true – at least as true as a Jack Tale oughtta be...

It's been a while since this *sitch-u-ayshun* happened, an', like some tales, it's been a little contrary gettin' this 'un all sorted out. Some tales is like 'at up here in the High Country. In this here tale, that was what happened. Jack done tol' me about takin' Angelo t' the back country waterfall within a week after it happened, an' I b'lieve what he told me. When it comes to his dog Angelo, Jack don't even hardly *"exaggerate."* But, it turns out not even Jack knew all that happened. So I d'cided t' dig into it m'self – with Angelo's help. An' now that Angelo's 'fessed up,' I reckon it's time t' tell y'all this tale. I hope y' like it.

"Angelo," said Jack when he took his dog into the back country off the far end o' Turtle Post road that first spring Angelo lived with Jack's fam'ly , "this is *some* country. I'm glad y' come with me, not only 'cause it's so purty, but also 'cause I can enjoy it better when I don't' have t' watch out fer the bears. Ever' time I been up here, 'cept in winter, I've seen bears – or at least seen signs of 'em. And now, comin' out o' hibernation, them bears'll all be hungry and they'll have the big head. We'll have t' have a caution."

Angelo's ears perked up at the mention of bears. After all, that was the reason Mr. Nate brought him t' Cove Creek Camp a few years before. Angelo wadn't a great big dog like what you'd think of as a "bear-despisin' dog." But he come from a long line o' workin' dogs—some o' y'ns know about them dogs—and when it come t' *people-pr'tectin'*, Angelo was all in! He made that very plain when he faced off against the boy bear who wanted t' make Jack his breakfast. Even if Jack had said nothin' as they started t' the back country, Angelo woulda known he needed t' be on the lookout fer critters, and he loved it!

"Look here, Angelo. Over yonder in the brambles -- see that footprint? And that leeetle bit of black hair?"

Angelo was thinkin' so loud, Jack could hear 'im. "See it? I could smell it a quarter mile back!"

"Don't get too excited, boy. I know I don't have t' worry about them bears with you around. Come on. Stay with me. It's about t' get intrestin'. They's a waterfall comin' up here in a little bit. Can y'smell it? It's so fresh and clean, I reckon it smells like Creation! Why, it ain't just cold and clear, it's *alive*! When y'get t' drink from it – you'll never want t' drink anywheres else—not even from a deep cove well! This waterfall is *satisfyin'*—you'll see. I cain't wait, boy. How 'bout you?!"

Angelo couldn't wait neither! He was so excited his tail was waggin' like a whirlycopter ready t' take off!

Now the Appalachian mountains are plumb populated with waterfalls from Georgia all the way up t' Maine, and here in the Blue Ridge, they's a passle of 'em. Big falls, like Amicalola at the southern end of the Appalachian Trail, double falls, like Anna Ruby, Cascades and Slidin' Rocks, waterfalls that let y' stay dry while y'r walkin' right underneath of 'em, and waterfalls that ain't hardly been seen n'r named 'cause they's so remote. That there's the kind of falls that brings us this tale.

Wellsir, in a couple o' shakes, Jack and Angelo could hear the falls, and in another minute or three they could see it and smell it. By the time they reached the base, felt the spray, and took a drink, the cascades had touched all o' their senses. Both Jack and Angelo thought they'd reached Heaven for sure!

After pausin' t' take it all in, Jack and Angelo began t' work their way up the side of the cascades. "C'mon, boy! Let's go on up t' the top. It ain't too steep. If it gets too tough, I'll carry y'."

Jack rec'nized Angelo's shorter legs and that some o' the rocks *he* could get up were kindly tall for Angelo. But they kep' goin', an' Angelo proved he was an amazin' climber. After a short spell, they come t' a small section o' the cascades that was a little flatter, an' the water wadn't rushin' s' fast.

"Let's stop here fer a spell, Angelo. See them rocks out in the middle? They's big enough t' stand on. Let's go out there." Jack started wadin' over t' the rocks.

Now they's somethin' y'all need t' know about traipsin' around in the woods in the spring. Ary high country boy knows that y' gotta have a good pair o' boots t' wear in the springtime. Jack had his on an' he was just fine in that creek – didn't have no problems with slippery rocks on the creek bed. Problem was, Angelo didn't have nothin' t' pertect his feet. Let's just say he wadn't quite as sure-footed navigatin' that creek. River rock and gravel was as bad on his feet as those metal grates they have for people t' walk on at Amicalola. Bein' in the middle o' the creek, it was slippery, too.

An' then it happened. Angelo lost his only foot hold, got caught up in a hole where they was an eddy swirlin' like a cyclone, and that spinnin' water threw 'im out the eddy and started t' carry him down stream. He was so startled, he barked at Jack.

"I'm excited, too, boy," called Jack without turnin' around. "C'mon."

Angelo sounded off again, "Jack – somethin' ain't right. Little help here?"

By the time he turned around, Jack saw Angelo bein' carried downstream. He didn't panic, 'cause they was still in a flat part of the cascade, but in a few shakes, his dog'd be headed down the next section o' the falls. Jack knew he had t' get to 'im as fast as he could. Even a cove dog would have a time of it further downstream.

"Angelo! I'm comin'! Y'all will be ok!" Jack was doin' his best t' run t' Angelo, but the water was just deep enough and fast enough t' make it hard – plus that spring current was getting' kindly cold.

"Jack! I don't like the look o' them falls comin' up." Jack was still hearin' Angelo-talk, then he lost track o' him as Angelo slid through some big rocks and on down a 7-foot drop.

Headin' t' the bank, Jack clambered down the side o' the cascades just in time t' see Angelo pull himself out o' the water downstream on the other side. He looked ok, but he definitely wadn't happy. He was soaked an' disoriented. He shook himself a few times while Jack was comin' across the creek. The water was deeper here, an' it slowed Jack down.

"Angelo!" cried Jack. "Look out!" Comin' out the rhododendron was a bear cub that had been watchin' the whole thing. Bein' a young'un, that cub had nary a thought o' causin' trouble – he was just curious. But, bein' a cub in the spring, Jack knew its Mama was close and was watchin' too. Trouble was, Jack slipped and fell, fillin' his boots and britches and accident'ly gulpin' a couple o' mouthfuls o' that cold runoff. When he come up, he was coughin' so bad he completely lost sight o' Angelo. He barely made it back t' the creek bank. Jack didn't know what was goin' on for the next hour or so.

Meanwhile, on the other side o' the creek *(and this is the part o' the tale that didn't surface 'til Angelo became shall we say "persuaded" t' fill me in on the "meanwhile." But y' gotta promise not t' tell Jack the whole tale. Let Angelo tell 'im.)*

Meanwhile, even in his disoriented state Angelo knew the bears was there. And, bein' a protective dog, he knew he needed t' do somethin' – if he didn't, they was danger lurkin' -- for himself, for Jack, and maybe even for that cub. His lineage through his great-great grandpa Pepper give him courage and a strong set o' protective instincts; his Mama Sallie Mae taught him leadership and compassion.

Angelo needed the courage, Jack needed the protection, and even though he was a "bear-despisin' dog," that cub needed t' be led.

Angelo didn't hesitate. He carefully, but confidently, moved toward that cub, watchin' the rhododendrons t' see when its Mama would show herself. Under his breath, he said, "Jack, I shore wish y' was here. An' I shore wish Pepper was here. I could use some o' his courage. But he ain't. F'rgive me, Jack, but I gotta do what I gotta do. If we's gonna be safe, I gotta get that cub back with his Mama. An' if that Mama bear don't take kindly to it, I swear on *my* Mama's life that I'm still gonna do ever'thing I can t' get back t' you an make sure you get back safe t' Brooks Cove."

When he was only a couple o' walkin' sticks distance from the cub, Angelo was near thrown on his back by the force of the Mama bear's charging roar. But it were curious – she never slapped at him, never even touched him; but they was no mistakin' the force behind that sound.

"Pepper, fire me up." Angelo got back on his feet and stood firm. He didn't bark at Mama bear; he didn't growl at her; he didn't even raise his hackles. He just stared. Sallie Mae would a' been proud o' her boy.

An' then he looked at the Mama bear and said, clear as he could, not knowin' if she'd understand, since he'd never had no truck with bears: "Here's y'r young'un. You best teach 'im t' mind his distance. Ain't ever'thing in these mountains is friendly."

"Don't need no friend. C'n handle trouble on our own." Mama bear was standin' firm herself. "Set my own cub straight -- protect him m'self and correct him m'self. *And*, it wadn't f'r you, dog."

Still standin' firm, Angelo challenged, "What wadn't for

me? I stared down bears before. Don't mean I got t' despise 'em. I'm from a long line o' protectors, an' m' instincts are on alert when I don't know what t' protect from."

Mama called back to 'im, "M' *roar* wadn't fer you. 'twas for that boar that was creepin' close. M' cub was d'stracted – just bein' a cub – an' you was still comin' out o' the falls. Neither of y'all even *heard* that boar. He was certain sure up t' no good. Don't like them filthy pigs, and I don't want 'em near m' fam'ly. Better for 'im t' jus' skedaddle. Ain't got time t' deal with my wayward young'un, a dog, and a boar that's got the big head. Now, go find y'r boy. Ain't no dogs like you come up here without their boy."

Angelo recognized that, just like over in Cove Creek Camp, he had a 'understandin' with this bear family. Without sayin' anything more, he headed back t' the creek, but he went upstream along the bank t' avoid that eddy where he first got in trouble. He crossed back over the creek and kep' lookin' f'r Jack. Fin'ly Angelo found him back downstream – shivery, wet, and still coughin' a mite. Jack looked awful.

"Jack, are y' ok? Let's get y' movin' to warm up. We got a ways t' go t' get back home. If sundown comes an' we's still out here, it ain't gonna be any good."

"I'll be ok, Angelo. I'm powerful glad y'r back. I was all dithered, not knowin where y' was. Are y' ok? I thought I lost you! Was y' hurt in the falls? Did y' run off that cub? I know his mama was close by, did y' have t' scare her off, too? I knew y'all would take care o' us, even when I lost sight o' you."

"Once I come out o' the water and saw the cub, I knew I had a job t' do," said Angelo. "And, I knew I couldn't rest till I found you. I'm ok, it was a *ad-venture*. You *love* ad-ventures, Jack. C'mon, we got t' get movin'. Ain't nobody else out this far in the back country. It's just you and me, and it's gettin' colder."

Jack and Angelo started back down the trail. Both of 'em was near give out. "But what happened?" Jack asked. "I lost y' fer a while – till y' showed up just now."

"Things ain't always like it seems they'd be, Jack. It just took a while. It's all good," said Angelo. "I got shook off, and took care o' the bears so's they wouldn't come after us. I learned from my own mama how t' herd critters t' where y' want 'em t' go. And, since I didn't want t' get caught in the eddy again, I went upstream t' where it was easier t' cross the creek t' get back t' you. And now I know y'r gonna be ok – if we c'n keep you movin'. My job ain't done yet, Jack. It's cold. We're both wet. C'mon. We got t' get movin if we're gonna get home."

Jack wadn't satisfied. "Angelo, they's somethin' y' ain't tellin' me. What really happened?"

"I had a job t' do, Jack. It'll all be good once't we get back home." Jack knew Angelo wadn't gonna say nothin' else 'bout what happened. He didn't know why. Important thing was, he knew he could trust Angelo. His fam'ly and neighbors up in the Cove had taught him y' cain't get along without trust.

It were a long walk back t' Brooks Cove, it was cold, and both Angelo and Jack was plumb wore out. After a while, Jack stopped – he felt like he'd give all he had t' give.

"I gotta stop, Angelo," said Jack. "I got nothin' left. And I know with all y' done t' pertect me from them bears and help me get movin' toward home, you must be give out, too."

"We can make it, Jack," said Angelo. "Rest here a minute. Then we go again till we got nothin' left. And then we do it again – puttin' one foot in front o' the other till we get home."

"Thank y', Angelo," said Jack. "Y' sound like Uncle Pap, tellin' me t' keep puttin' one foot in front o' t'other."

"It's good advice. Uncle Pap sounds like a good man," said Angelo.

"He is. And I'm also glad we was at the waterfall with its special water. Drinkin' it made me feel like I was more alive, and I know it made us stronger so's we could get back t' the Cove."

"Me, too, Jack. Me, too," said Angelo.

"Angelo, you got the best o' ol' Pepper *and* o' your mama Sallie Mae! I'm so grateful – y' saved me again. But y' gotta promise me that someday y'll tell me what else happened out there by the waterfall with the bears."

"Let's us just work on getting' home first," replied Angelo.

Angelo had his reasons for not wantin' t' talk about the bears and the boar. Maybe it was 'cause at the time, he was still kinda new t' Brooks Cove, and comin' from Cove Creek Camp, he had a "bear-despisin'" reputation t' pertect. Maybe he was embarrassed b'cause he didn't know the boar was there – they ain't quiet, an' he'd messed up. Maybe it was 'cause he didn't want Jack t' think he'd let 'im down. What I *do* know is that my speculatin' ain't worth much, 'cause like Angelo said, things is seldom what they seem.

I reckon some day Angelo'll 'fess up t' Jack. Till then, we got t' be content knowin' they got home safe and had lots of other *ad-ventures* an' *sitch-u-ayshuns*.

Jack and Aslan's Roar

Y'all ain't gonna b'lieve this, but it's true...

And unlike other tales I done tol' you, it ain't *"at least as true as a Jack Tale oughtta be"* – it's true. Jack didn't have t' tell me nary a thing in this tale – I was there! Just ask anyone in the Cove – they was *all* there t' witness the events of this tale.

Now, b'fore we go anywheres w'this tale, I got some

whatchacall full disclosure. First, about the picture y'all see: it ain't a catamount. It's a African lion. I know that. I ain't tryin' t' pull one over on y'. Second, I know that catamounts don't roar – they scream, kindly like a kittycat. Iff'n y' ever heard a cat scream, y' know the cat's distressed. But when y' hear a *lion* roar, y' know somethin' else is distressed. In this tale, Aslan the catamount – he roars. The Tale, the picture, and the roar are true. Pay 'tention. You'll see.

It was early spring, just after the equinox. Jack was itchin' to get out in the mountains at night. This time of year was perfect t' see sights in the moonlight y'all cain't see any other time. It was kindly chilly up in the High country, but Jack and Angelo was used to it.

"Angelo!" Jack called. "Let's us go fer a walk out in the moonlight. It don't get any better 'n this. The light's perfect, and folk up here in the Cove has always said y' might see some 'unusual' sights. Who knows, we might even see Aslan out on patrol."

Angelo's ears stood up, his eyes lit up, and his tail was goin' a hunert mile an hour. He'd been around Aslan many a time, an' he literally looked up t' 'im. Whenever he thought about Aslan's patrol, he thought t' hisself, "I done that self-same thing, watchin' out fer bears, over in Cove Creek Camp for Mr. Nate!" Angelo, the "bear-despisin', people-pertectin' dog" couldn't a'been more ready!

"Let's go, boy." Jack and Angelo took off acrost th' cove road and headed over toward Aslan's cave. "Maybe we'll see 'im , Buckshot." (Jack sometimes referred t' Angelo by the same nickname that Jack's daddy Lee called Jack. It always made 'im feel good t' say the name "Buckshot.")

Sure enough, before they got t' the hills beyond Arrie's

garden, here come Aslan, and in the moonlight, he seemed a little different. He was alert, like tonight's patrol was somethin' even more important than usual.

"I've been out on patrol since dusk. Somethin's different tonight. I've got a bad feeling about the Cove tonight. Seem like they's evil tryin' t' make its way here. I know how you love y'r ad-ventures, Jack, but tonight it's best iff'n you and the dog keep your eyes and ears open." Aslan continued, 'specially t' Angelo, "Jack done tol' me that what y'r best at is bein' all in when it comes t' protectin' your people. You c'n smell things they cain't; you c'n hear things they cain't, and you've got a job that no one else can do. I know what that's like." And for emphasis, "I hope I'm wrong about evil tonight. But Angelo, *you* gotta be all in." And instantly, Angelo *was* all in.

Aslan continued on patrol, while Jack and Angelo continued around below Arrie's place and on up toward Doc Blevins' place. Doc seen 'em comin' and come out t' meet 'em.

"Ev'nin', Jack. Ev'nin' Angelo. What brings y'all out on this fine ev'nin'?"

"Ev'nin' Doc. We been hankerin' fer a night t' get out. Cove folk like you have been tellin' me since I was a littl'un how special things look in the light of the Easter moon. But Doc," Jack seemed less excited and more anxious, "We just saw Aslan, and he seemed worried. He was on patrol, but he wadn't hisself. Said he felt some kind o' evil out tonight. He even put Angelo on alert."

Doc looked square at Angelo, serious, not excited. " 'R y'ready, boy? Ready t' help Aslan p'rtect the Cove?"

Now, Angelo don't talk t' just anybody, but he talks t' Doc Blevins. "Doc, me an' Aslan trust each other." Angelo continued, "When he says be ready, I make m'self ready fer whatever's comin'. Y'know me an' my kin – we always been ready to give whatever it took, even if it meant our life, t' do our job o' protectin' our people."

Doc knew the stories. "Thank you, Angelo."

About then, they heard a scream that could only have come from a catamount. It was from over off Turtle Post Road, and sounded like it was comin' down from the meadow where Jack had found the owl. Angelo was off like a shot, with Jack on his tail. Doc was doin' his best t' follow. When they come to a clearin' just up above the Cove Road, they started hearin' other, shall we say "unusual" sounds – sounds they never heard before. Not even Angelo knew what they was, they was so eerie.

One by one the Cove folk came out of their homes and was hurryin' up t' Turtle Post Road t' see what was goin' on. The sounds had turned into a babel; most of it was so strange that nary a soul could make anythin' out, but Jack and Angelo could pick out Aslan's growl in the middle of it. They wanted t' rush t' he'p him, but Doc held 'em back.

"Son, Aslan was right. They's evil up 'ere. Th' ain't nothin' any o' us can do. We gotta let Aslan handle this 'un. He signed up fer such as this." Still, it was nigh onto impossible t' hold Angelo back. He said t' Doc, "Doc, I gotta go. I signed on t' protect Aslan, too, not just Jack an' his people."

"I know," said Doc. "But this 'un's beyond you. I just hope it ain't beyond Aslan."

Evil *was* in the air – folk was unaccustomed to feelin' it up in the cove. But what they witnessed that night, they would never forget -- and they'd never completely comprehend it neither. What I do know, 'specially lookin' back on it, is that it was not t' be a silent night.

Aslan was stalkin' somethin'. Jack couldn't make it out.

Seem like one minute y' could see somethin' and the next minute they was nothin' there. It like t'confuse 'im – he was growlin' and shakin' his head, sometimes kindly whinin', an' that big catamount let out more'n one scream that'd freeze y'r blood. The sounds the evil thing made seem t' come from a hundred places at a time. Cove folk was froze, both fearful and compelled t'watch at the same time. And then it seemed like it all b'come crystal clear to Aslan. He stood up and spoke:

"Y'r not welcome in this cove. BE GONE!"

It were a command the likes o' which nary a soul this side o' heaven ever heard b'fore. They was a flurry o' scattered light. Aslan, tempted t' chase the lights as if they was the Kuykendall's kittens, stood firm.

"IN THE NAME OF ALL THAT'S HOLY, BE GONE!"

At once the evil came all t'gether and its eyes met Aslan's. In the unearthly light of that rising Easter moon, a battle commenced. Aslan, committed t' protecting the cove from outside predators, wondered if he'd met his match. This foe clearly wadn't a critter these ancient mountains sheltered. Aslan'd dominate over any mountain critter and in a heartbeat he'd a'thrown their bones t' the vultures. This 'thing' – whatever it was – was other worldly, kindly like the Brown Mountain Lights, but pure evil. As the battle got fiercer and fiercer, Aslan was transformed into an oversized African lion instead of the catamount whose eyes Jack first saw in the cave.

Each inflicted what ever'one o' us thought was mortal wounds on the other. Each faltered and fell. Each rose up again, determined that there would be one more round t' the battle. And that same full moon that led the Israelites out o' Egypt t' escape the angel of death revealed the foe lunging at the big cat's feet, intendin' t' upend and cripple him. But Aslan showed his cat-like determination, rose up, and came down on that unearthly being, crushing its skull. The sound of that blow filled the cove, but what came next was so startling that it shook the very foundations of the mountains.

It was Aslan's roar. The roar of the victor announcing a final victory over its foe. And it was so loud, so forceful, and so commanding, it was not of this world. Now, the folk who study animal sounds say that the roar of an adult male lion can carry up to 5 miles, but this one seemed like it penetrated from the heights of these mountains that overshadow the cove, to the depths of inner earth itself.

The battle was over. Aslan was spent. Completely. It was all he could do t' jus' lay on the ground. Cove folk was stunned. Some o' us cried out in fear that we'd lost 'im. Some went runnin' to 'im. Angelo was the first t' reach Aslan, but by this time, he'd quit bein' a African lion and was hisself again. "Aslan! Are y' all right? Look like you nearly died!"

Aslan raised an eye whisker. "I did Angelo. I did die – at least as a African lion. But God brought me back – as a catamount -- after I finished off that unearthly evil. I finished that evil off, Angelo."

Jack come up next, "But you was bleedin', Aslan. I never done seen you bleed. I never even saw you hurt! Are y' gonna be ok?"

"Son," Aslan mustered, "I'll be ok again. Just not now."

"Aslan, alls I can say – for all o' us up here in Brooks Cove – is Thank You. Fer savin' us from that evil," said Mr. Lee.

"For riddin' us o' that evil thing for all time," added Doc.

And one by one us other cove folk added our thanks.

Miss Dayle, Stormy, Arrie, Lacey and Nehi, Farmer King and his family, Mr. Israel, the Kuykendalls, Maw Padgett and her young'uns, an' Mr. Justis's family all come up t' Aslan t' congratulate 'im on his victory and thank 'im for savin' the cove – and each one o' us. And one by one we started to cheer an' praise "our" catamount.

And on that next Sunday, Easter Sunday, they was an Easter meditation read at church. Nobody knows who had wrote it, but they asked me t' read it. I was proud t' represent Brooks Cove with a new – and very personal – understandin' o' Easter. Oh – one thing – it ain't wrote in "dialect." Seemed more reverent that way. An' the folk o' Brooks Cove wanted y'all t' have a copy of it. Happy Easter.

Easter Meditation

It was *not* a silent night, not like the one thirty-some years before.

Instead of a *chorus of angels* there was weeping;

> Mary, His mother, who wept with joy on the night He was born

> Now wept again at His death. Yet not hopelessly.

Instead of *calm* there was confusion;

> His death was incomprehensible, though a part of the Father's plan from the Beginning.

Instead of the *brightness* of a star to guide the way,

> The light of the heavens disappeared for hours.

Blood –His blood -- was on the ground, the blood that would redeem us and sanctify us.

And even though it felt (*even to Him*) like God was silent on this *unsilent* night

He was actively at work ensuring that we could echo "Glory to God in the Highest" and give thanks

--to Him – for our own invitation to spend eternity praising Him with loud --

> Even rowdy, rambunctious, and grateful praise to Him

> > for Whose pleasure we were created

> > > and in Whom we live and breathe and have our being.

And so SILENCE is not in order on this Holy night.

For on this night the roar of the Lion of Judah – heard throughout all of creation –

Proclaims Victory over sin and death!

> For all who will accept that victory

> > For all of eternity!

And He shall reign forever and ever.

> Hallelujah!   Amen!

Jack and the Piebald Ridge Deer

*Y'all ain't gonna b'lieve this,
but it's true – at least as true as a Jack Tale oughtta be...*

"Hey, Jack!" Tom Kuykendall saw Jack walkin' down the Cove Road on a bright Saturday mornin' in early April. He was one o' Jack's friends in Brooks Cove. "Mr. Justis told me t'other day that they's a piebald deer over on the ridge at the back end o' the cove. What's a piebald deer?

Ain't got nary a hair on its head? Does it go around stealin' pies? Wild cherry's m' fav'rite."

"Hey, Tom. I like Mamaw Eulagene's Macintosh Special apple pie," replied Jack. "She's got a couple o' trees at her home place. Piebald? Naw, it ain't bald. I remember Mama and Daddy sayin' they saw a piebald deer over on Piebald Ridge b'fore I was born, but I never seen one. Mama said it was real unusual – big brown spots on a white background. Daddy said the 'pie' part comes from the magpie – you know, kindly like a crow but with big white patches on its wings, and the 'bald' part comes from lookin' like the brown is on a white background. Mama said it looked like a goat."

"A goat? How can a deer look like a goat?" Tom was surprised.

"I dunno. But Mama thought it was purty," said Jack. "She said 'twas curious, though – when she tried t' tell other folk about the deer, all they heard was 'Piebald Ridge.' Said it was almost like she'd said 'haint' or 'spook.' No one – in the Cove or off – 'd listen t' Mama or Daddy, so they kindly quit talking about the piebald."

Now don't let y'r britches get shortchanged – Iff'n y' don't know what a haint *is, y'll find out direc'ly.*

"I ain't never seen a piebald deer – or a haint – if y' c'd see such a thing," said Tom. "Y' wanna go see can we find one? Sounds like a 'ad-venture.' I see y' already got y'r stick an' a tote with y'r lunch."

"Sure, Tom. I'm ready t'go. But as much as I've roamed around this Cove and these mountains, I ain't never been t' a place called Piebald Ridge."

"Me neither. Let's us go ask Mr. Justis how t' get there. He knows ever'where in these mountains," said Tom. "Mama said his fam'ly's been here forever!"

So off they went, down the road a short piece from Tom's house. They found Mr. Justis on his porch, fixin' t' leave f'r the day.

"Hey boys. Air y' up t' somethin'? Whatcha got planned f'r the day?" Mr. Justis grew up in Brooks Cove an' he liked Jack and Tom. He wadn't young and he wadn't old, but he was old enough t' have his own fam'ly and t' be called "*Mr.*" by Tom and Jack.

"Mr. Justis," said Jack, "we want t' go lookin' for that Piebald deer you tol' Tom about, but we don't know how t' get t' Piebald Ridge. Can y' tell us where t' go? We done already got our walkin' sticks and lunches."

"Well," said Mr. Justis. Then he paused. "Boys, it might jest be squirrel chatter that they's a piebald deer over on th' Ridge. That tale's been runnin' around since before either o' y'uns was born. *And*, folk say Piebald Ridge is spooky. You sure y' want t' go over there? It's a far piece. Y'r Mamas know that's where you want t' go?"

At the same time Tom said, "Yessir" and Jack said, "Kinda – I mean I think so."

"Jack," said Mr. Justis. "You go back home and let y'r Mama know where you wanna go. AND, let her know you need t' take y'r dog Angelo – IF y'r Daddy can spare 'im for the day. Iff'n y' don't do that, I ain't gonna tell y' how t' get there."

"Is it on the way?" asked Jack.

"No. Y'll have t' backtrack a bit. Y' wanna know how t' get there 'r not?"

"Yessir. I'll go tell her, *and* I'll grab Angelo, too. Daddy'll be done with 'im by now. Then we'll come right back."

"ASK her, Jack – don't tell her. You're wantin' a favor. You know what MaMaw Eulagene says about favors."

"Yessir. I'll ask her. We'll be right back."

Fifteen minutes later, Jack, Tom, and Angelo was back at Mr. Justis' porch. "Mama said that since it was you who said we needed t' get permission she figgered it'd be ok." Jack continued, "Then when she found out we'd have t' take Angelo, she said she KNEW it was gonna be all right. And as I was runnin' back t'meet Tom, she holler'd somethin' 'bout solvin' a old mystery. You know anything about that?"

"Possibly." Mr. Justis looked deep in thought. He give Jack 'n Tom directions t' get to Piebald Ridge and wished 'em "Godspeed." Jack thought it was a little strange, Mr. Justis sayin' "Godspeed" an' all. Made 'im wonder if there *was* somethin' dangerous over on Piebald Ridge. But he decided t' not worry; Mr. Justis never steered 'em wrong, and he *was* the one person they could trust t' give directions a boy could 'preciate and follow.

* * *

"Boy, Mr. Justis was right," said Tom. "It IS a far piece t' the ridge. I hope seein' a deer that looks like a goat is worth it." They'd only gone 'bout a mile and a half, but it was rougher terrain than if they was on th' ol' loggin' road *and* th' ridge was real remote. "I thought they'd at least be a trail up this mountainside," panted Tom. "Alls we seem t' get is rocks 'n roots 'n gullys."

"C'mon, Tom. You ready t' turn back now?" teased Jack. "You that tard or you thinkin' 'bout the rumors o' haints over there?"

"Course not," Tom shot back. "*Unusual* is one thing; *worth it* might be a whole 'nother thing. It's certain-sure as remote as Mr. Justis said it was. I c'n see why if there ever was a safe spot where the deer wadn't hunted this'd be it."

"Well, it'll be worth it whatever it turns out t' be," said

Jack, tryin' t' calm Tom. "Like you said, it's a *ad-venture*, Tom -- t' someplace we ain't never been before. AND, we got the whole day, *and* we got Angelo." Rubbin' his dog's ears, Jack said, "You won't be 'fraid o' no haints, will y' boy?"

Angelo didn't say nothin' – he still wadn't sure if he should talk around Tom. *'Course I wouldn't be 'fraid o' no haint. I done stood down bears b'fore – even a mama bear with a cub -- and I got a job t' do!'*

After 'nother mile 'r so, they were reachin' the ridgeline. The forest seemed a little darker, but it was dotted with mountain dogwoods at various stages of flower – some were still kindly creamy color and others that were further along shined in the scattered sunbeams that broke through the canopy. When they got t' the "bald" part o' Piebald Ridge, they felt right at home. Jack had a run-in with a coyote a while back on 'nother bald – he called it a 'meadow' cause he liked that word. But this bald was different. Only thing on *this* bald was rhododendrons scattered around on the rock faces an' a line o' sarvisberry trees at the far end o' the bald out from under the canopy. They was in full bloom, brilliant white and as downy as Mr. Israel's goslins.

"Tom," drooled Jack. "We GOT t' come back in a couple o' months t' pick sarvis berries. Those trees'll be loaded! They're even better 'n the blueberries in the cove – AND we won't hafta fight the bears for 'em." Tom had t' wipe his chin on his sleeve he was salivatin' s' much! The bald *was* purty, and with the sarvis berries -- neither Jack n'r Tom saw ary reason *Cove* folk'd think it was spooky.

All sudden-like, Jack noticed that Angelo was standin' dead still, tremblin' just barely. He'd been trackin' those deer for the past half mile, makin' sure Jack and Tom found their way t' see 'em. Angelo looked almost like he was pointin'. Then Jack saw the piebald. He had t' fight his voice t' not cry out in surprise an' excitement.

"Tom," Jack whispered. "Over there – in the thicket. Y' c'n barely see it. See it?"

"I think so, Jack. Wait. It moved. Now I c'n see it." Tom was gettin' wide-eyed.

"Well, I'll be!" 'xclaimed Jack, still in a whisper. "Mama was right – It *does* look like a goat. Farmer King had a few goats a couple o' years ago, and they looked like 'at. 'Cept this deer is near full grown."

"It ain't a fawn, and it ain't a haint, certain-sure!" Tom was gettin' 'cited 'imself. "Can we go any closer – y'know, t' see it better?"

"Let's try. But we gotta be slow, y' cain't be jerky – and most of all, we *cain't* seem scared OR 'cited. The deer'd run sure as a August fog if we were."

Since the "haint" and "spooky" rumor had spread over the years, they was 'most never *anyone* out on Piebald Ridge. So, as Jack, Tom, and Angelo got closer, the deer were mostly just curious, not ready t' raise their white tails. When they were within 100 yards, Jack 'n Tom could see that they was at least 3 deer – 2 of th' normal forest-litter brown color and the one piebald.

"Jack," said Tom. "Do y' think they're gonna run?"

"Dunno. Sometimes I've been able t' get right up on deer up in the High Country; sometimes they bolt. I never seen a piebald, so I don't know what she'll do. But the other two look a little fidgety, like they was pr'tectin' her." It was clear that Jack had some 'sperience with deer. "Let's keep goin'. Careful-like."

Angelo started creepin' closer and closer, like he was on a mission. Out th' corner o' his nose, he sniffed a familiar smell and turned his nose up t' the left.

"Jack. Tom," said Aslan. "What are y'uns doin' up here on the bald?"

* * *

Tom nearly jumped outta his boots. Aslan, the Cove's "adopted" catamount, had snuck up on 'em. Jack was surprised, too, but he knew better'n t' show it.

"Aslan! Y' scared me half t' death. Don't go sneakin' up on a body like 'at."

"I'm a cat, Tom," replied Aslan. "I ain't in the habit o' makin' noise."

"We was tryin' t' get a better look at that piebald deer," Tom continued, pointing across the bald. "We ain't never seen one b'fore."

"Mr. Justis tol' us they was a piebald deer up here on Piebald Ridge," added Jack. "When we asked how to get up here, he said he'd tell us, but we had to be sure that our Mamas knew where we were plannin' t' go. AND, he made us promise t' bring Angelo with us."

"Mr. Justis is a wise man – he was lookin' out fer y'uns." replied Aslan. "Y'r outside the cove *and* outside the boundaries o' my usual patrol. But, I *do* come t' this Ridge often. I reckon Mr. Justis knows that."

Tom and Jack looked at each other.

"Surprised?" asked Aslan. "Just 'cause it's outside the Cove, don't mean it's off limits t'me. T' be completely clear, I hunt over here."

"What?!" Tom was shocked. "I thought y' promised t' pr'tect the cove."

"I did," stated Aslan. "This ain't part o' Brooks Cove. Cove only comes as far as the hill where you had t' take a rest, Tom."

"How'd you know about that?!" exclaimed Tom.

"I agreed t' pr'tect the people and critters o' th' Cove. That includes you, Tom, and you, Jack," said Aslan. "Y'r daddies ain't th' only ones who keep track o' y'uns. But I decided t' keep my eyes on y'all b'cause you don't know this Ridge, an' I do. Sometimes they's things up here that even Angelo might want help with. 'Sides, sometimes I get hungry f'r deer meat."

Tom looked like his ears was connected t' a steam engine!

"B'fore y' get worked up, I made a sacred promise t' pr'tect th' cove an' its critters," continued Aslan. "I know about th' piebald deer. I ain't never took one o' them."

For the first time since Aslan came out o' his cave t' become part o' Brooks Cove (*an' that's another tale*), Tom and Jack didn't know what t' make o' him. Jack's brain was spinnin' s' fast, he was dizzy on overdrive.

In his head, Jack started t' wonder about Aslan. *"Helpful? Certain sure. Truthful? Without a doubt. Loyal? No question – he even risked his life pr'tectin' us back in the Easter moon, an' he has th' scars t' prove it! In spite o' that, is he a wild cat – not really tame? I know I trust 'im, an' so does Mama. But would Aslan harm us or the piebald?*

Fin'ly takin' a breath, Jack turned t' Tom: "Alls I c'n say is I'm glad Angelo is with us." Then t' Angelo, "Whaddya think boy?"

"I think iffn we're gonna get a better look at that piebald, I better start herdin' her t' where y' c'n get closer." Angelo was on a mission an' he didn't care if Tom c'd hear him 'r not. "An' we gotta figger out what t' do with that young buck that's with her."

"How d' y' know it's a buck, Angelo – he ain't got even nubby antlers."

Angelo just looked at Tom. "I got a dog's nose, Tom. He smells like a buck, not a doe."

Tom was flat embarrassed. Aslan just smiled. "C'mon, Angelo. Let's get started."

So Aslan and Angelo started creepin' 'cross the bald, their eyes glued on the deer. It had a freezin' effect on th' deer, so they kep' on getting' closer. Angelo kindly peeled off t' the left toward the sarvisberry trees where he could come in behind the deer. He knew his great-great grandaddy Pepper'd be proud o' him, Pepper bein' a cattle dog an' all. Angelo knew Jack was watchin', and he knew Jack had learned from his Daddy how t' work a herd dog. So when Angelo got t' the tree line, he stopped t' wait for Jack's signal t' herd the deer.

Meanwhile, Aslan kept creepin' straight toward the buck. Closer he got, the more the buck stayed froze.

"Son," called Aslan, "We don't mean y' no harm, nor the piebald neither. M' friends just want a better look at her – they ain't seen one so purty as her b'fore."

The buck called back with his best bravado, "Why in the name o' the Ridge d' you think I'd trust you – a catamount, of all things!"

Still creepin' forward, Aslan replied, "Accordin' t' the Ridge, you'd be a fool t' trust the word o' such as me. I might be hungry, but I don't lie, an' I don't give bad advice. One o' my ancestors has a debt t' pay t' one o' that piebald's ancestors. We ain't gonna harm ary a one o' y'all."

"Do you think y' c'n catch me? They's a reason m' grandbuck tol' ME t' stay by the side o' the piebald t' pr'tect her."

Now Aslan was annoyed. He knew this'n was jus' bein' a young buck, but he also knew the buck needed a straight-up lesson. He stopped an' stared right through th' eyes o' that young buck, darin' him t' challenge again. "Mebbe y'all *could* outrun me, and mebbe y' c'd outflank that dog that done snuck up closer than anyone ever got t' you. But I done tol' you that I'm hungry, an' I know *I* wouldn't want t' mess with a dog that's stood down a mama bear lookin' out f'r her cub. I know this Ridge better'n anyone else. Y' cain't hide like the haints y' pretend t' be -- ain't no moon out t'night. And I know plenty o' people over in Brooks Cove who'd love t' have a new hat rack made of whatever antlers you think y'll grow. I'm patient. So are m' friends. Alls they wanna do is see the lady a little closer."

The young buck backed down – f'r now.

About this time, Jack signaled Angelo t' 'cut the piebald outta the herd' so she'd be away from the others. Silently, and quick as spring runoff, he had her movin' toward Jack.

"Ma'am," said Angelo to the piebald. "You are a beauty! Can m' friends take a closer look? Mr. Aslan already checked with your buck over there, an' by th' looks of it, now he's ok with us takin' a look."

"When I heard that cat say he had a debt t' pay t' my ancestor," said the piebald, "I knew we c'd trust y'uns. But please be careful."

Angelo signaled Jack it was ok, and Jack signaled Tom t' come closer. "Tom," whispered Jack, "it's ok f'r us t' get closer, but we cain't get right up on her. She ain't the least bit tame. Take a look, remember what she looks like so y' c'n make a picture of 'er when y' get back home, then back away gentle-like. That buck's cooperatin' right now, but he's still a 'young buck' if y' catch my drift."

* * *

Mr. Justis had a change of plans and after a while, he d'cided to trail behind the boys on their way t' the ridge. He didn't know that Aslan was gonna head out there, too, but he wadn't surprised when he got t' the ridge and found 'em all there. He smiled when he saw Angelo herdin' th' piebald and Aslan schoolin' th' buck. Seein' all was as he hoped it'd be, he kindly waited till they come back across the bald. He'd heard enough o' Aslan's conversation with th' buck t' know that an ol' mystery was indeed bein' solved, like Jack's Mama had suggested.

When the boys and Angelo and Aslan said "thank you" t' the piebald, the buck, and the other deer and come back over t' th' ridgeline, Mr. Justis greeted 'em. "Looks like I missed th' party.

"Didja see her, Mr. Justis?" asked Tom. "It was just like y' said –there IS a piebald deer up on this ridge."

"I saw her, Tom. She's a beautiful creature certain sure. Angelo, Aslan, thank y'uns for givin' up y'r day t' be sure these boys'd be ok. I truly 'preciate it." Then, t' Aslan, "I had t' smile when that young buck fin'ly figgered out that he wouldn't have a leg t' stand on iff'n he kep' on challengin' you, Aslan." And t' Angelo, "Y' handled that piebald like she was y'r cousin, Angelo. You almost made me b'lieve y' c'ld herd cats!"

Angelo and Aslan looked at each other, then nodded t' Mr Justis. "It's our honor, Mr. Justis. Not ever' one shows how much they care f'r the boys like you do," said Aslan. Angelo smiled s' big it stretched clean across the bald. He added, "We had a job t' do."

"Like Jack's mama hinted," continued Mr. Justis, "they's some mysteries startin' t' bust open, an' seems t' me they's all kindly connected. Aslan, the first one concerns the debt your ancestor owed t' the piebald's ancestor. Seems y'r ancestor had been avoidin' a certain hunter all day long about 15 year ago. It was the end o' the month, and as night was comin' on, the blue moon rose big and full. Catamounts wadn't common f'r hunters t' hunt, seein' as how the deer population in the Blue Ridge was still comin' back from near extinction 50 year ago at the turn o' th' cent'ry. But just as the hunter was ready t' draw a bead and shoot him for food, that hunter was distracted by what he saw as a haint floatin' across this same bald. He was scared half outta his wits, and took off back down the ridge line. Turns out that "haint" was one of the piebald's ancestors. Bein' pale colored, she looked like a ghost. Y'r ancestor was saved by the piebald's ancestor, and even if she didn't know she was doin' the savin,' I reckon you just paid that debt."

"Much obliged," said Aslan thankfully. "I'd heard some o' that story, but I didn't know it was savin' m' ancestor from a hunter. I'm doubly glad they wadn't a real haint and that you didn't shoot m' ancestor OR the piebald.

"How d' you know that story, Mr Justis?" asked Jack.

"I was that hunter," stated Mr. Justis. "It was a hard spell f'r m' fam'ly, and we needed food. Plus, my niece, Remona, was stayin' with us for a spell when her Mama and Daddy had t' leave Cincinnati b'cause o' some trouble over 'cross th' river in Kentucky. Catamount's a big critter. It woulda fed us fer a long time. But the Lord provided other game f'r us and we made out OK.

"What about the debt owed by th' piebald?" asked Tom. "Was it to a buck?"

"No, Tom, it was to m' niece Remona. She had wandered up t' th' ridge th' night b'fore the blue moon while she was stayin' with us. She had her 15th birthday that day, and she was so dreamy like about "comin' of age" that she just took off. It was late at night and I'd already gone t' bed, 'cause I knew I had t'go huntin' the next day so we'd have food the next week. A garden can only go so far, y'know. It was her that first saw the 'piebald haint', and when she got back home, she told me and m'wife an' ever'one she c'd find that she saw a haint up on the ridge where the piebald deer live. So, th' next day, after huntin' all day with no game and the blue moon comin' out, I was tard and frustrated. Then I thought I saw a piebald deer under the sarvisberry trees and woulda shot it for food, but I looked again an' it was gone – disappeared right out from under m' eyes. Looked again, saw the big cat, and when it rose up t' try t' threaten me, the deer bolted an' I seen the haint. I ain't backtracked that fast ever since."

"Jack, I only put it all together just today after y'r Mama said somethin' about solvin' mysteries. I saw her just as I was crestin' the Ridge. Seems like the mystery o' the Piebald Haint is why folk kindly quit talkin' t' her an' your daddy for a while. Even if I ain't the one who started the rumor about th' piebald haint, I'm powerful sorry. I'll see her tomorrow after church t'pologize."

"Mr. Justis, you done paid any debt y' think you have t' Mama years ago, you bein' such a good neighbor an' lookin' after Tom 'n me 'n others here in th' Cove."

"Folk done looked after the Justis fam'ly f'r generations here in these mountains," said Mr. Justis, "It's the least I c'n do.

"Aslan," continued Jack, "they's just one other thing. I want t' ask a favor o' you.

"Ask," said Aslan. "I reckon you done earned the right t' ask."

"The favor is that y'll pr'tect the piebald."

"Are you sure y' know what you're askin', Jack?" broke in Mr. Justis. "This ain't th' cove, an' ever'one knows catamounts eat deer meat. Like Mamaw Eulagene says, be certain sure y'r not askin' a whatchacall 'trivial' favor NOR a favor that's bigger'n the askin.' Are y' sure 'bout this'n that the askin' is worth the grantin'?"

"Yessir, Mr. Justis, I b'lieve I'm sure." Turnin' t' Aslan, "We've always give an' took from one another, Aslan, an' I think we're kindly even. So I ain't afraid t' ask. Like you said t' the buck, no one knows Piebald Ridge as well as you. We both know they's lots o' deer up here and they must be other areas you hunt that have deer. Alls I'm askin is that you kindly pr'tect any piebald deer you see, or at least don't hunt 'em. An' if I'm still on th' short end o' the stick, mebbe y' c'ld think y'r doin' it f'r Mama. She thinks they're purty. AN' she thinks th' world o' you, Aslan."

"Y'r right, Jack. We've both helped each other from th' first time we met. And y'r not on the short end o' the stick." Aslan paused, then simply stated, "Agreed. I won't hunt any piebald, and I'll even pr'tect 'em. Now we need t' get back t' Brooks Cove. We done used up ever'body's day, and y'r fam'lies are gonna start wond'rin' where y' are. Plus, it'll be dusk in a couple o' hours, an' I got Cove Patrol comin' up."

Just as they were leavin', Tom leaned over t' Jack an' said, "Ain't that y'r Mama hurryin' down the trail over there? Didn't Mr. Justis say he saw her leavin' t' go back t' th' Cove?"

"He did f'r sure. I wonder what she was doin' up here." Jack didn't know what t' make of it.

"D' y' think she was spyin' on us?" asked Tom.

"Dunno. I'll bet Aslan knows about it – but he'd never tell us anything."

* * *

About a week later, Remona surprised her Uncle Justis (as she called him) with a visit.

"Remona!" exclaimed Mr. Justis. "What a surprise! I'm prouder'n a peacock t' see y' up here in th' cove! What brings y' here?"

"Uncle Justis," she replied, gettin' all leaky-eyed. "I've been thinkin' about how special the Cove was to me when I was a girl, and just needed a Cove fix. I asked Mama to help look after my family so I could come up here. So, I took a couple of days off work and drove on up "t' the first house on the left as y' enter Brooks Cove."

After learnin' about the events of the past few days and the mystery solvin' up on Piebald Ridge, Remona said "Uncle Justis, I don't feel right about you apologizing for something I started, even if I didn't mean to start it. That 'piebald haint' rumor put people at odds for way too long. It's time it ended. I need to go see Miss Dayle. Where do you think I could find her?"

"She'll likely be over at the Farmer's Market –it's jus' 'cross th' road. It's a right nice place -- Miss Dayle's boy Jack started it just after he met that catmount they call Aslan – but that's a story f'r another time. C'mon Remona, let's go find 'er. 'Sides, I reckon I oughtta tell her that I know she was over at th' ridge last week t' be sure the boys was ok, and that I wouldn't a 'spected anything else. I know it's been a while, but you'll love her like y' did when you was a girl visitin'."

Sure 'nuff, Miss Dayle was there, and she was thrilled t' see Remona. They talked, and Miss Dayle allowed as how she knew they was a good reason f'r her t' keep silent about the Piebald haint all those years, but she never knew what that reason was. It was as if the Lord tol' her t' not worry -- it served His purpose f'r her; so, she d'cided t' not worry. Remona and Miss Dayle got right w' each other quickly, then Miss Dayle brought our Narrator into the conversation (he was a regular at th' Farmers Market in Brooks Cove and was easy t' find – AND he was always lookin' f'r a story).

"Miss Remona," asked Narrator, "What draws y' to th' Cove after 15 years bein' away? I kindly gather y' didn't come just t' 'pologize to Miss Dayle."

"No, sir," answered Remona. "As I was telling Miss Dayle, this place is special to our family."

"How?"

"Wellsir," she started.

Heads up -- High Country dialect wadn't nat'ral t' Remona, her havin' grown up in Cincinnati. Even so, she's as real as a crocus in the snow.

"There's even more to the story than what you already know. Now that I've got my own family, I've been looking into our family history through geneology records when I can find them, and right here in the High Country, it goes back over a hundred years, and part of the story goes back even further than that."

By now, both the Narrator and Miss Dayle were captivated, neither of 'em expectin' t' hear such rich fam'ly hist'ry.

"One of our Justis ancestors -- my Uncle's family didn't used to have a family name but after what I'm about to tell you they got inspired by Sojourner Truth to take on 'Justis' for their name. Anyway, this ancestor originally left an unnamed Southern plantation with his wife and young son in the late 1850s. Their route took them to Greensboro where the family was sheltered briefly by Quakers and then led by an educator named D. Austin who was headed up to the mountains -- NC, VA, TN – he wouldn't tell anyone just where he was going for safety reasons. He thought the understory of the back country would be suitable shelter for the Justis family. Mr. Austin's ancestor had hidden out in the High Country from the British 80 years earlier at the time of the Revolution and, though it was a hard life, it was better than being subject to the Crown. Now it was his chance to "pay it forward," like so many other 'conductors' on the Underground Railroad."

"The Justis family made their way at night through the gap that would become Brooks Cove and pushed on to Piebald Ridge, where the forest had overtaken all attempts at settlement. The ridge had been home to very few people, mostly Cherokee, but lots of wildlife, especially deer – so many deer that rare as they were, the piebald were seen every year and it came to be called Piebald Ridge."

"The family grew, but had such a desperate need for shelter that they were almost never seen by anyone. They struggled for the next several years, living off the mountain, using the skills they picked up out of necessity, and "the Lord's provision." Finally, in the spring of 1866, they crept out of their mountain sanctuary and learned that President Lincoln had abolished slavery. They were free!"

"Unfortunately, free didn't necessarily mean safe, and they made a hard decision to travel further north to be able to start over, vowing that one day the Justis family would return to Piebald Ridge to make a home. That dream finally came true with my great grandpa (Uncle Justis' PaPaw) when he re-settled in the Cove 60 years ago. Your neighbor, my Uncle Justis, was born and raised in this cove, and what I just told you is why he is so emotional about Piebald Ridge. It's his home, and he considers it to be his ancestral home, too. The cove has been such an important part of my family's history that I get emotional about it, too. And like

15 years ago when I was coming of age and saw my own piebald deer (even if I got spooked and thought it was a haint), I had to come back to the Cove and the Ridge just to connect with family history and roots. Just being here makes me feel somehow more complete."

Hearin' a story unfoldin', other folk at the Farmer's Market had come a little closer just t' listen. Over in th' corner Jack had snuck in and quietly made his way over t' his mama. When Miss Remona finished, 'specially by sayin' th' Cove made her feel complete, they was clappin' from all over th' market.

Miss Dayle looked up, her eyes glistnin'. "Remona, thank y' f'r honorin' us with your fam'ly hist'ry. Y'all have made *us* more complete, too -- they ain't a person here, why, nary a person who ever even *visited* Brooks Cove that y'r uncle didn't help."

Jack piped up, "Miss Remona, iff'n y' want t' go back t' th' ridge, we done saw a piebald over there just last week. Me 'n Tom 'n Angelo 'n Aslan worked out a 'agreement' with her an' th' others. Aslan 'll pr'tect 'em and she – meanin' th' piebald – she'll let us come take a closer look at how purty she is. If y' wanna go, we'll take y' over there. I'll even get y' a walkin' stick."

"Thank you, Jack. I'd love to go out there before I go home."

* * *

They's things a culture'll teach y' iff'n y'r willin' t' pay attention. Sometimes the lesson ain't learnt right away. Sometimes what y' learn don't come from who y' would've expected it t' come from. And sometimes, even if it ain't dramatic, a lesson can still be profound.

Jack and the Leaves of Three

Y'all ain't gonna b'lieve this,
but it's true – at least as true as a Jack Tale oughtta be...

"Mr. Israel?" asked Jack.

"Hey, Jack. What's on y'r mind?" Johnny Israel is Jack's next-door neighbor just down the Cove Road from Jack's family.

"Comin' back t' the Cove from wanderin' up toward a

ridge line a while back, I saw what looked like an ol' fire tower over yonder. So I took Angelo an' went back up there a few weeks ago t' see could we find it. But we got d'stracted pickin' sarvisberries and hurryin' t' get back, we didn't see hide n'r hair of it. You done lived here in th' Cove since you were young -- you ever seen it?"

"Not f'r a long time. It's still standin', what's left of it. But the forest threatens t' cover it up a little more ever' year." Mr. Israel continued. "When I was a young'un, my brothers took me up there a few times. They was older 'n me and liked causin' trouble. One time I remember they tol' me there was a treasure up on top, but y' had t' climb out t' the edge o' the platform t' get it. Said it was silver, and they dared me t' climb up an' get it, so I did. When I got out t' the 'treasure', alls I saw was a stick o' gum. They loved t' make fun o' me'."

"That was mean," said Jack, "But I guess you showed 'em by climbin' all the way up there to look!"

Mr. Israel had always liked Jack. After his wife Lisa died 10 years ago, he sometimes was lookin' f'r an excuse to have an *ad-venture* with a young'un. "How 'bout you an' me an' Angelo go find it on Saturday after y'r chores 'r done?"

"You mean it? That'd be better'n pie on Tuesday! I'll ask Mama t' make us lunches we can eat on top o' th' tower. I'll get m' chores done early, and Angelo 'n me'll be by on Saturday morning 'bout 8:30. Do y' need a walkin' stick? I'll bring y' one."

"I've got my own walkin' stick. It's th' one I made with y'r daddy b'fore you was born. Been waitin' f'r a *ad-venture* t' use it again. Thank y', Jack. See you on Saturday morning."

Just as Jack was leavin', Angelo come runnin' up just a

grinnin'. Jack petted an' hugged 'im all over. "You hear that, boy? We're gonna have a *ad-venture* with Mr. Israel on Sat'rday mornin'!"

* * *

Saturday morning, Jack was covered with poison oak. He could hardly move, an' he itched s' much he'd scratched some o' the blisters open and they was red an' raw.

When Jack didn't show up by 8:45, Mr. Israel come by t' see was he ok.

Miss Dayle come t' the door. "Jack got the poison oak, Johnny. It ain't the first time – prob'ly got it from Angelo."

"I'm not s'rprised," smiled Mr. Israel. "T' other day when Jack come t' ask me about the ol' fire tower, just b'fore leavin', Angelo come up and Jack was rubbin' him all over. You know how boys are, Miss Dayle, Jack must've got it on his hands 'n arms – prob'ly spread it all over!"

Mr. Israel had been a friend for nigh on 20 years; they was in school together, along with Jack's daddy Mr. Lee. It had been heartbreakin' when Johnny lost his wife t' the leukemia after havin' been married f'r only 6 years. An' they never had no young'uns o' their own.

"I'll go round up some jewel weed 'n bring it by. There's always some close to a poison oak patch. Alls y' gotta do is crush the stem and rub the juice onto the sores. Works better'n medicine most o' the time. Even Doc Blevins recommends it!"

"I 'preciate it, Johnny," said Miss Dayle as he took off t' the forest behind his house. "Jack wanted t' know could y' go t' the fire tower one day next week?"

Mr. Israel called back over his shoulder, "Let's try f'r Wednesday afternoon. He should be a lot better by then, an' with school bein' out, we'll both be able t' go." Mr. Israel was a biology teacher.

* * *

"Sorry about Sat'rday, Mr. Israel. I couldn't move, I was so covered over with the poison oak. Thank y' f'r the jewel weed and f'r lettin' us go t' find the fire tower t'day. I'm a lot better and I'm 'cited 'bout lookin' f'r treasure!

"Me too, Jack. I ain't been on a *ad-venture* f'r a while. They's a couple o' things I hope we find t'day – one of 'em *is* treasure. But first we got to go find a patch o' poison oak like what Angelo got into."

"I don't want to find no poison oak patch, Mr. Israel! I've had my fill o' that nonsense!" Jack couldn't even stand t' think about poison oak.

"Do y' know what it looks like?" asked Mr. Israel.

"Course I do. Ever' good Cove boy knows poison oak. You know the sayin', 'leaves o' three, let it be.'"

"That's for poison ivy, Jack. Poison oak don't always have 3 leaves." Mr. Israel was a little surprised. "B'sides, when we find a poison oak patch, there'll likely be jewel weed close. I guess it's God's way o' providin' a antidote close t' where we get into that mess o' irritation."

As they was gettin' closer t' where he remembered the fire tower was, Mr. Israel spotted a patch o' poison oak. Angelo was walkin' right through it!

"Jack," he said, liftin' a couple o' leaves with the tip o' his walkin' stick. "Here it is. Take a good look at poison oak. That way at least *you*'ll know enough t' stay out of it. Looks like y' cain't do too much about Angelo, so we better look t' see what the jewel weed looks like. There's usually a patch close."

"Is that it, Mr. Israel?" asked Jack. "What does it really look like?"

"Most people call it Jewel weed b'cause when y' put its leaves under water they look like they's covered with jewels. Some folk call it touch-me-not b'cause when y' just barely touch the flower, it spits its seeds at y'. The flower is orange 'n spotted. Look – over here. Here's some."

"That's purty, Mr. Israel. Can I pick some?"

"You better! Y'r likely t' need it. Angelo's been all through the poison oak today, an' knowin' you, you'll f'rget an' get it all over y'sef. Break off some o' the stem, then go rub on Angelo, bein' careful to touch 'im just with y'r hands. Crush the juice outta the stem an' rub it on y'r hands; it has a compound that'll neutralize the poison oak oil. Then wait. Y' won't get the poison oak this time."

Jack did what his neighbor tol' him t' do. After 15 minutes, he still didn't get the poison oak. "Well I'll be! Thank y' Mr. Israel!"

"Y'r welcome, Jack. It also works on poison ivy, poison sumac, an' stingin' nettles. Now, with that taken care of, let's get t' the best part of this ad-venture – the Treasure!

* * *

"Jack – Look. Look up. What d'y' see?"

"Is that the fire tower? Is it the one y'r brothers dared y' t' climb?"

"The self-same one. See the platform up 'ere?" Mr. Israel pointed up with his walkin' stick.

"C'n we go up t' th' platform, Mr. Israel?" Jack was itchin' to climb.

"Hold on, Jack. We best test t' see if the steps 'r still strong enough t' climb." Mr. Israel investigated. "Seem's ok, Jack. Let's go, careful-like."

They both climbed up. One flight, a second flight, a third flight, and then up a narrow ladder t' the platform.

The surrounding trees had grown so much since Mr. Israel was called *Little Johnny* that by the time they got t' the top, they felt like they climbed clean through the understory!

"Wouldja look at that view! I c'n see the coyote meadow over yonder, 'n Doc Blevins' homestead at the top o' the Cove and a whole lot more!" Jack was excited!

"Wadn't near so overgrown last time I was up here. Careful, now, pick y'r way over here t' the edge o' the platform." Mr. Israel encouraged Jack out t' the place where he'd been as a boy. "Here's where the 'chewin-gum' treasure was."

"I'm still mad about what y'r brothers did t' you way back then," said Jack.

"Jack – y'gotta let some things go. B'sides, after a while, I come back up here by m'self and found a much better treasure from this self-same spot. They's TWO treasures. Y' done already found one of 'em."

"Y' mean the view? That IS a treasure, Mr. Israel. In fact, this view'd give a lifetime o' memories about Brooks Cove. Thank y' f'r bringin' me up here."

"There's more, Jack," said Mr. Israel. "Drop y'r eyes 'n look over t' y'r left just a shade. Look out about 50 feet from the base o' th' tower."

"What is it, Mr. Israel?" Alls Jack saw was green ground cover.

"Look again, Jack."

"Is there some jewel weed here, too?" asked Jack. He truly didn't want the fire tower t' be in a poison oak patch.

"Poison oak ain't up here, Jack, or at least it wadn't when the fire tower was bein' used. Rangers made sure o' that."

"How'd they do that? Burn it off?"

"No, Jack. If y' burn poison oak, the irritatin' oil goes

up with the smoke and if y' get smoke on y' – or worse, if you breathe it, y'll get poison oak just the same. It's another reason f'r 'leaves o' three, let it be.' Also y' cain't just dump herbicide on it. When it rains, or if animals eat it, then the oil ain't digested and it just gets into the ground water or food system."

"How'd they get rid of it?"

"Probably used somethin' like salt water. Salt'll kill a plant pretty quick. Back to the treasure. It *is* flowers, but not jewel weed. Do y' see little white or purple spots?"

"No. Wait -- now I see 'em. What is it, Mr. Israel? Wildflowers?"

"They're called *trillium*, Jack. Another plant that has *leaves* -- or flowers --*of three*," said Mr. Israel. It reminds us of the Holy Trinity – the Father, Son, and Holy Ghost. You've heard the preacher talk about them b'fore."

"Yessir, Mr. Israel. I just didn't know they was a flower for the Trinity. Are they holy flowers?"

"Sort of, Jack. God made 'em so they're a special reminder o' the Trinity. That's treasure enough, dontcha think?"

"Can we take some back t' Mama? She'd love 'em."

"It'd be better f'r you t' bring her up here, Jack. As pretty as they are, the flowers'd wilt b'fore y' get home, an' if y' try t' dig some up to transplant at home, y'd have t' wait at least a year b'fore they'd flower and they might not grow at all. Plus, unless y'r on private land–an' this fire tower ain't on private land--trillium is a protected plant – it's illegal t' dig it up. It's yet another meaning for *leaves of three, let it be*. Just remember that up here y' got a special reminder o' how God made the 'flowers of the field.'"

"Thank you, Mr. Israel. I'll always remember that you cared enough t' heal my poison oak, that you took time t' show me where t' find the jewel weed, and the trillium flowers, and that y' showed me a place that's special t' you. Always."

"Thank you, Jack, f'r goin' on a *ad-venture* with me an' f'r wantin' t' see some o' what makes Brooks Cove home. It's been right nice – like y' said last week, better 'n pie on Tuesday!"

Jack and the Home-Grown Apple

Y'all ain't gonna b'lieve this,
but it's true, at least as true as a Jack Tale oughtta be...

Jack's Daddy, Lee, sometimes like t' think that the apple don't fall far from the tree. It's a common thing for daddies to think – we take pride in it. Now, y'all might be thinkin' that if Lee said "The apple don't fall far from the tree," he was talkin' about Jack and how they're a lot alike.

Listen careful-like, this here tale is goin' t' take a turn or two.

Remember how Jack's daddy Lee took the family on a campin' weekend and Jack got into a *sitch-u-ayshun* with a teenage boy-bear? Then you'll remember that Jack, actin' like a teenager himself, would never have got *himself* out of trouble – somebody else had t' step up and cover his back. That somebody was Angelo – the "camp-protectin', bear despisin' dog" who "*had a job t' do.*" Y'all know that a little later Angelo came t' live with Jack's fam'ly. Wellsir, this here tale is, shall we say, "The Rest of the Story," but it comes to us not from our own Brooks Cove but from Greene's Gap, where Lee's cousin's neighbor's uncle once't removed on his Mama's side– I can see by your eyes that this is gettin' way too convoluticated – I cain't keep it straight myself most of the time. Anyway's, they was a cattle ranch up in Greene's Gap, and Lee was well acquainted with the ranch.

'Bout a week ago, when Jack done finished his chores for the evenin', he was talkin' t' his daddy. Since Angelo had a habit of 'helpin' Jack with the chores they was talkin' about him.

"Jack," said Lee, "Did I ever tell you about Greene's Gap Cattle Ranch?"

"Yessir," said Jack. "You told me that it was a big operation with a 'legacy herd' of black angus and that they supplied only the finest of the finest steaks t' the Grove Park Inn over in Asheville. You also said it was spell-bindin' t' watch their main dog Pepper work the herd so's he could protect 'em. I wish I coulda seen him do his stuff on that ranch."

"It *was* a sight! You'd have loved it, certain sure," said Lee. "Pepper warn't no special breed – he was just the best cattle dog *anyone* had ever seen. When a cow was bein' ornery and keepin' the herd from gettin' to where it needed t' go, why Pepper would nip at her flanks t' "motivate" her. Usually that meant he was likely to get kicked or stomped on. But Pepper didn't mind – *he had a job t' do*. When the herd had t' spend the night in a cove the other side of Greene's Gap, Pepper made sure that the bears didn't help themselves t' a steak or some ribs. He wasn't a great big dog, like a mastiff or some other foreign breed, but he had a great big spirit, and puttin' hisself between the bear and the herd – well, let's just say that even when he got beat up, Pepper made sure that the bear didn't get what he come for. Again, he didn't seem t' mind – *he had a job to do*. And when a storm was brewin', like it often does in the High Country, Pepper would be sure the herd got to a protected area even if it meant he was the last one gettin' to safety himself. At least one time that I know of, ol' Pepper got struck by lightning! I think he *did* mind that one, but -- say it with me Jack --

Jack chimed in, '*He had a job t' do.*"

"That's right." Lee smiled, pleased with Jack and his interest. "More 'n once Pepper got shot at; more'n once, he had to stand down a catamount; more 'n once he had t' run off would-be thieves. Why if he hadn't been a dog, people woulda called him Chuck Norris!"

Jack laughed. He'd heard some of the rumors about Chuck Norris.

"Why, I reckon Pepper coulda even herded cats!" Lee exclaimed. Then, going on, "He was amazin,' certain-sure. But son," Lee continued, "Pepper ain't the star of this story. I kindly kept track of him over the years, and followed his blood line best I could. I wanted t' be sure t' know if one o' Pepper's kin showed his own mastery of herdin'. About 10 year ago, I heard about someone over in

Lester Cove who had a small sheep farm and a dog that kept the place safe. Stories I heard made me wonder if that dog was related to Pepper. I did some checkin', and sure 'nuff, it was one of Pepper's great granddaughters."

"Now, I didn't know nothing about herdin' sheep, so one day when I had t' make a run to Asheville, I went lookin' t' see could I see that dog in action over in Lester Cove. I got an education in herdin', and as *brave* as Pepper was as a cow dog, SallieMae was *smart* as a sheep dog. Y'see, herdin' sheep ain't about *motivatin'* a wayward sheep, it's about keepin' the sheep from turnin' wayward in the first place. SallieMae was better'n excellent at it! She worked with the shepherd – and often by herself, t' *lead* them sheep where they needed t' go. When she done that, there was no kickin' nor stompin', there was no need t' hide from bears or catamounts 'cause SallieMae wouldn't have led the sheep where they wouldn't have been safe. And sure as August fogs there was no hidin' out in a storm waitin' t'get struck by lightning. SallieMae's life was dead on easy compared to Pepper's."

"Daddy, is SallieMae still alive and workin'? I'd love t' see her. And, I bet Angelo would love t' see her, too. You done told me y'self that Angelo is a natural herd dog."

"No, son, she passed a few years ago because of heartworm. She *woulda* loved t' see Angelo, though, cause – and I never told you this – Angelo was one of her pups. I kindly followed her pups also, just like I did with Pepper's, and when Mr. Nate was lookin' for some dogs t' protect Cove Creek Camp, I give him a heads up that he couldn't do better than gettin' one of SallieMae's own. So he did. Then when we went up there t' the family campin' weekend, you remember how I said it would be good for us t' be there?"

"Yessir."

"What else did I say?" asked Lee.

"You said you had …. Now I get it," said Jack. "You said you had your reasons for us goin.' Was you settin' us up?"

"I wanted t' get a look at how you and Angelo would get along. If it went well, I was gonna be on the lookout for another of SallieMae's pups that we might get hold of for our family."

"But Mr. Nate done give him to us – to me," said Jack. "Did he give him from his heart? Or did you buy Angelo?" Jack was gettin' depressed now, wonderin' if Mr. Nate's motive was pure.

"He just give him to you," said Lee. "Wadn't no one more surprised or grateful than me. Mr. Nate's a genuine good neighbor."

"But they's another thing that both Pepper and SallieMae knew how t' do – and as far as I know, Angelo knows it, too – and that's how t' not give in to a distraction."

"What do you mean, Daddy?"

"I mean, that when you *'have a job t' do'* (as Pepper and Angelo would say), that you don't let anything steal your focus. What woulda happened if Pepper had started watchin' a squirrel or chasin' a deer when there was bears around? Or if SallieMae had took off because she heard a dinner bell whilst tryin' t' get her sheep into the fold? And what woulda happened if Angelo had sat down t' scratch a flea when that teenage boy-bear was comin' after you?"

Jack was silent, thinkin' about what his daddy said.

"It's a real question, boy. What woulda happened."

"Nothin' good. Prob'ly a disaster," said Jack.

"You're right. Prob'ly a disaster," said Lee. "Like, a *you-wouldn't-be-here* disaster. It's never the distraction's fault.

It wouldn't be the squirrel's fault, it wouldn't be the dinner bell's fault, it wouldn't be the flea's fault. The disaster wouldn't be their fault. But it still would be a disaster. Now how could you avoid the disaster?"

"Don't get distracted?" asked Jack.

"Don't get distracted," said Jack's Daddy. Pushing him further, "How ya' gonna do that?"

"By not payin' attention t' anything 'cept the job?" asked Jack.

"And by *anticipatin'* what you have t' be prepared for. You didn't know it – I made sure of that – but when you was out chasin' around with that Catamount – without Angelo, I might add -- I was never out of your sightline. I had t' be sure you wasn't walkin' into something I couldn't handle. I was *anticipatin'* any trouble you might get into because you got distracted."

"Wait a minute, Daddy. Are you tellin' me that you've been watchin' me all the time on all my ad-ventures?" asked Jack. Now he was startin' t' feel disappointed, as if his daddy didn't trust him t' grow up.

"No, sir, son." Said Lee. "Only sometimes. Other times I knew you'd be o.k., cause I knew somebody else had your back or I'd seen you in similar situations and you had your own back. I cain't bear the thought of losin' you, son, but even more, I cain't bear the thought of you not growin' into the man you're gonna be."

"Daddy?" asked Jack. "You know the old saying, 'the apple don't fall far from the tree?"

"Yes, son."

"Well, if you're the tree, I want t' be the apple."

Acknowledgments

This collection of stories would not have been possible without the support of my family, the wisdom and insights of my friends Charlene DeWitt and Evelyn Asher, the willing feedback from members of the Tall Tales Writer's Group on drafts of the stories, and from family, dear friends, and colleagues over the years who shared interesting experiences, pithy sayings, thoughtful comments, and much appreciated encouragement.

Special thanks goes to my publisher, BookLogix, for their deep and practical knowledge of the publishing industry that has made this book a reality, and whose grace-filled encouragement got me started, kept me going, and celebrated its conclusion. 'Thank you' clearly doesn't come close to expressing my gratitude.